Birds

of

Vice

&

Virtue

Want To Catch Up?

To my father.
After you were gone, I finally understood.

"Through my travels...I try to take righteous steps because...right or left could mean life or death."

~Rakim

Chapter One

TOR GLANCES OVER HIS shoulder at the girl on the couch. His girl-friend...or something like that. With a sigh, he places down his knife and rubs his hands off on his apron. His stomach was doing flips, and his hands were shaking.

"Ja—" he stops himself before calling for her. *What would he say? What would she think?*

'I lied.'

It was a white lie. A soft one. It was so easy to reverse. Tell the truth, and the truth shall set you free. Right? Practice what you preach and all that jazz.

He clears his throat and steps further through the kitchen archway.

"Jaamini."

She turns the TV down and looks at him with furrowed brows. A crease dips between them, twisted with her face.

Tor rolls his shoulders and lifts his chin.

I lied.

"Food's almost done."

She smiles. "Alright. When you're done, we should eat in here."

Tor glances at the TV, his chest deflating.

'The news.'

She was still watching it. An explosion in Las Vegas took down the Palms Casino.

Terrorists. That's what they called it.

He looks at her worried face. The reflection of light in her shiny hazel eyes. With a frown, he returns to the kitchen and finishes cutting the lettuce. He needs to tell her. Just not now. She's too scared...and so is he.

He made a promise to stay with her. To stay safe until the heat was off, until something bigger buried their crime deep in the dirt. But he would break that promise.

Once he's finishes making their bowls of salad, he places them on the coffee table by her feet. She gingerly sips from her steaming cup of hot cocoa with an unwavering gaze.

"You alright?"

She glances to the side, then down into her M&M mug.

"No...But I will be. What about you?"

He clears his throat.

"I'm alright," he says. He smiles and she smiles back.

The two let silence fill the air between them.

'Just tell her.' He thinks as she returns to the news and disregards the feel of his gaze on her skin. Tor sighs and grabs the two plates of grilled cheese and grits.

She sits up when he places the hot plate on top of the pillow in her lap.

"This looks amazing! How'd you learn to cook?" She asks. Picks up the grilled cheese topped with eggs, bacon, and tomato and stuffs her face.

His smile falters, and he stuffs a bite into his mouth.

Jaamini raises a brow.

"Right. You most likely have a quote for that. Let me think..." She scrunches her eyes closed and leans side to side, humming.

"Got one." She says. Her eyes bulged and she grinned.

Tor keeps chewing to disguise his laughter.

"What?" He asks, finally swallowing a very dry bit of bread.

"A true magician—"

"Nope." He cuts in. He shakes his head feverishly. "No way. If I'm cooking, what does that have to do with magic?"

She bursts into laughter, curling up into a ball, gasping for air.

He knew she was just joking to lighten the mood. They were in a precarious place, not knowing if they'd get caught. Not knowing if they were truly hidden away here in this safe house.

"You're going to choke love, get up," Tor says.

He pulls at her shoulder lightly until she is sitting straight up against the couch cushion.

Her face is flushed, and she wipes at the tears gathering in her eyes.

He absently mimics the smile spreading over her face. "I learned from my mom." He says.

Jaamini nods and takes a bite of her sandwich.

Tor ignores her soft sigh and flips the channel. They finish their food quietly while watching cartoons.

"Do you miss her?" Jaamini asks.

Tor wipes his hands with a handkerchief and then wipes around his mouth. He passes one to her, and she does the same.

"No." He says.

She places her plate on top of her empty bowl. "I miss my mother in a way. But she was never truly good to me." Jaamini says.

"What did she do?" Tor asks, turning his body towards her.

She twists her hands through her blonde curls. Her nails are bright and yellow with dainty daisies painted on them. Her dress is thick, knit, and hugs tightly to her figure.

"Among other things, she ran away from home one day and abandoned me in a field of sunflowers."

He opens his mouth but closes it just as quick.

"I was so tiny then, that I couldn't see over them. When the sun went down, I slept on the ground until my grandfather found me in the morning. He had the entire academy searching for us."

"Academy?" Tor asks.

Jaamini turns to him. She pulls one of his hands into hers, tracing the patterns of ink over his skin.

"My grandfather ran an orphanage, it doubled as an academy for...gifted children."

"Gifted?" He repeats.

Jaamini chuckles dryly and squeezes his hand.

"Retarded, disabled, mentally unstable, or physically weak. But it was just code for a training ground to breed killers. None of us have servere disabilities."

"I didn't know you had one."

She shrugs. "I don't just go around telling people," Jaamini says.

He pulls her hands up and kisses the back of each.

They smile at each other for a minute. Just one quiet minute, they are content. Content with the low murmur of the TV, the light purr of the heater, the soft white flecks of snow falling from the clouds, and with the person sitting in front of them.

A knock startles them, making them break apart and stare down the hall. It starts again, but this time three long rasps against the door.

Jaamini frowns, worrying her pink-tinted lip between her teeth.

"It's my dad. I got it," she says.

Jaamini rushes down the dark hall and pops open the door.

Pinky, her father walks inside, shuffling off his coat and hanging it in the closet. Tony, his assistant, steps in after him, rubbing gloved hands up and down his arms.

"Hey baby cuz!" he says. He pulls Jaamini into a tight embrace.

She hugs him back and points down the hall.

Tony, the blonde, waves before kicking off his boots and putting up his coat.

Pinky joins Tor on the couch, glaring at the dishes on the coffee table.

"Just stumble out of bed, did you?" he seethes.

Tor sighs, collecting the dishes.

"Sir, it's not like that." He says.

"Oh? You're living with my daughter," Pinky says.

"Under orders!" Tor whispers-yells, glancing down the hall. "For your information, I like to take things slow."

Tor passes by him. His heart jumps when Pinky's arm shoots out in front of him.

Pinky stands just inches above him and looks down into his eyes.

"I haven't forgotten you're a mole. Remember that I will kill you if anything happens to my daughter."

Tor swallows dryly, entering the kitchen. He drops the dishes into the sink. Heaving out heavily, he leans against the counter.

'Bastard.'

"I'm not scared," Tor mumbles under his breath.

"You should be," Tony says.

Tor jumps, reaching for his waistband, before he remembers he isn't even wearing his holster.

"You startled me," Tor says.

Tony shrugs, joining him in front of the sink. "He's not going to let you off so easily, even though you've proved yourself."

Tor shrugs. "How are your parents? Since the explosion and all that."

Tony leans against the counter. "They're good. Thanks to you guys, they got out unscathed."

Tor sucks his teeth, wringing his hands. "If it weren't for us, that explosion wouldn't have happened in the first place."

Tony taps at his phone, and Tor's phone buzzes in his pocket. "That's your pay. Use it wisely."

Tor eyes Tony warily before reaching for his phone and opening his banking app. His mouth falls open at the sheer number of zeros that follow after the twenty. He grasps his phone tightly, stuttering.

"Hazard pay. It's not from me, it's from the boss. Don't fuck up. No more siding with the Vipers or you'll get you and your mother killed." Tony says. His usually jovial tone was lost.

Tor's spit gets caught in his throat. Pressure weighed his shoulders down. Pressure wasn't good. Pressure makes him worry, and worry leads to mistakes.

"Can I—" He sighs and stops himself. "Thank him for me?" He asks Tony.

"Thank him? Nope, I refuse to do anything so vile. You do it when you report back tomorrow."

Tor hums a strangled noise and turns on the water. The instant he starts to wash the dishes, Tony is gone, off into a different part of the apartment. But the weight remains.

Chapter Two

THEIR VOICES FILTER IN through the walls. Thin, gray painted walls that tremble when they're loud, and thunder when they're quiet.

Tor turns the faucet off and dries his hands, joining the group in the living room. He presses his back into the wall and listens to their conversation.

"Sullivan will call you in for your next mission soon. You need to be ready to do things you've never dreamed of..." Pinky pauses for a moment to look at his daughter. "Horrible things." He says.

"If blowing up a building full of people is not horrible, then consider me shocked," Jaamini says. She folds her arms over her chest.

Pinky's lips pinch together, and he puts his glass down.

"I don't think you understand what signing up for this gang really means. We aren't just a street pack."

'You act like it.' Tor thinks to himself, holding his scoff.

"We are a family, family means mafia. And Mafia means business." Pinky states.

"I know. I grew up in Spain." Jaamini says, reminding him. She stands and joins Tor by the wall. Her small hand slides into his, and she gives a gentle squeeze.

"Have you finished raining on my parade?" She asks.

Pinky takes the shades from his face.

Tor's hands ball up.

Jaamini twitches by his side.

Shades on mean he's watching you, shades off means you're a target.

"Parade? We don't have time for theatric Mini. Things are being set into motion. Change is coming, and you...*you* will bring it." She gulps and squares her shoulders.

"Then let it come."

Pinky shifts his gaze to their joined hands, then up to Tor.

Pinky stands and waves him over.

Tor holds his breath. For a moment, a fleeting second, he doesn't move. Then he stood out of Jaamini's grasp, facing her father.

"You must be ready, *boy*. Thousands of people will die."

"Yes, sir."

Pinky places his shades back on and straightens out his shirt.

"And Tor?" He calls, rounding the couch.

"Yes?"

Pinky pauses, stopping Tony from walking behind him. He clears his throat and points.

"Take off the damn silky. You look like a street rat. Not a man."

Tor sucks his teeth.

Pinky raises a brow and inclines his head.

"With all due respect. Go to hell." Tor says.

Silence creeps between them. It swallows the space, pressing into their shoulders and sweeping around their feet. It creeps and creeps until it fills the room with heat.

"Ditto," Pinky says. He turns and heads straight for the coat closet.

Tony looks between the two until his neck snaps loudly. He groans and runs a hand over it.

Jaamini comforts him while hiding her laughter behind her hair.

"Listen, Tor, be careful," Tony says. He grabs Jaamini's hands to kiss the back. "You stay safe, and out of trouble, see you at the house."

"See you then," Jaamini says.

Tony scurries down the hall, taking his coat from Pinky and jumping into his boots. He looks back once to wave before closing the door behind himself.

"You really hate him?" Jaamini throws herself onto the couch.

Tor shakes his head. "No, I don't hate him, but he treats me like I'm inhuman. He's been at this longer than I." Tor says.

Jaamini puts her head on his shoulder, and they snuggle into the pillows. "You shouldn't let him rile you up like that. I like your durag."

Tor chuckles, running a hand over the ends of her hair. "Well, he's one to talk, he's like forty with a leather jacket, buzz cut, and a pair of shades."

She snickers. "You think that I was right to come here?" Jaamini asks after a moment of silence.

Tor lifts her chin, her eyes sparkling. One was more blue, the other more green. But they were equally shiny with hope.

'I lied.' He frowns and shakes his head. His thoughts snake in like venom.

"No, you aren't wrong for coming to claim your birthright. You're not wrong for following orders."

"But I'm wrong for killing, right?"

Tor shrugs. "To be honest, I don't know...if you're a sinner because you planted bombs, then I'm a sinner for letting you," he says.

Jaamini puts her head into her hands. Her sobs are light, like her skin, her eyes, and her hair. Her body shakes when she cries, and now it is no different.

She gasps and hiccups.

Tor pulls her deep against his side and kisses her forehead. She cries so hard for so long that tears soak through his shirt. This has been every night since that day.

Thanksgiving.

He sighs, turning the TV off.

"You should go get some rest. You'll be back at the job, so rest as much as possible."

She pulls away and wipes at her eyes. "Did you get paid?" She croaks.

He stands pulling her up to join him. "Don't worry about that. Let's get you right."

She follows him to the room at the back.

He stops in front of the door.

'I lied. The truth will set me free.'

"Mini," he says.

Jaamini opens the door and steps into the doorway.

"I get it, get washed up and go to sleep. Not like I just woke up or anything," she sighs and picks at her blue stress ball.

"Mini," Tor repeats.

"I just don't know Tor, I want to do right by everybody. But is that possible—"

"Mini!" Tor calls.

She jumps and blinks slowly.

Tor straightens out his coat and readjusts his suitcase.

The man looks him over with mock approval. "Yous leave little o' Avalon, and yous come back a rich man. So you switched up?"

Tor lets the man admire the gold watch on his wrist, the diamond studs in its face. The straight black trench coat and his gleaming dress shoes.

"I never switched up. What do you want?" he asks.

Juice comes to stand in front of him. "Man, I was checking on ya mom yesterday. She was high as a kite, kept talking bout how ungrateful yous were."

Tor pinches his lips together.

"Still wearing that, I see," Juice says, leaning in towards the silver chain hanging around his neck.

Tor absently grabs his Rosary and tucks it under his shirt. "What do you want, Juice?"

The man's eyes met his, and the color around his iris was yellow. His teeth were rotting. The front two had been cleanly knocked out.

Tor's hand twitches in memory.

"Just checking. Come down to the club when yous got time. Aight? Stop acting scary."

Tor nods once and clears the rest of the space up to the door. He checks the mail and pulls out a stack of envelopes. Then he checks the mat and pulls out the spare key.

'Scary? The only person acting scary was him, the way he always had those drooping eyes on someone. Always watching. Always waiting.'

Tor enters the house and locks the door. He places his suitcase against the wall and props his coat on top of it.

"Momma?" he calls.

His boots creak on the hardwood floors. The light flickers, and warm air circles him, trapped inside by closed-off windows and doors.

"Momma, it's Tor!" he says louder.

Pots and pans rattle not too far from him in the kitchen.

He approaches slowly, holding tightly to the collar of his shirt. He was holding his rosary, tucked away like a secret.

"Oh, Tor baby." His mother slurs. She takes another sip of her brown liquid, sloshing it around in her glass. The ice chips clink together.

The sour scent of piss wafts through the kitchen.

Tor gags covering his nose.

"Mama," he says softly.

She doesn't respond, just downs her drink.

"Marilyn."

Tor's mother turns her head in his direction. "Whatchu want, baby boy?"

"Why are you drinking so early, Mama?"

She slams her glass against the table and stands on shaky legs.

Tor moves to help her, and she halts him with her hand. "You ungrateful boy. Stop questioning me, I'm an adult!" she slurs.

Tor puts his head down, shaking it.

"Mama, come get in bed, and I'll make you some lunch."

She thinks about it for a moment, swaying side to side. Her deep brown skin flushed white in her knuckles.

Tor approaches cautiously. He peels her fingers from the corner of the table and wraps one arm over his shoulder.

"Miss you," she mumbles, putting her head of gray hair on his shoulder.

He smiles to himself and hauls her through the house to the back room.

"You still sleep down here?" He asks, glaring at the door.

"Yeah?" She pulls off of him, opens the door and steps inside.

"I know how to boy, go s' nice."

He tilts his head and waits to see what she does. Does he ask for clarification? *No. She's drunk. Probably high too.* Marylin climbs into bed and kicks off her heels.

Tor sighs and closes her door.

The sign hanging from its center sways and scrapes its surface.

Tor frowns at the name on the door.

'She should sleep in her room.'

Tor leaves her to nap. He plugs his nose with a clothing pin and grabs the disposable gloves from the top of the closet. His hands covered, and with his shoes discarded by the front door, he starts cleaning.

For a moment, a split second he is reminded of his past, when he pushed himself to scrub. Scrub every little thing until it gleamed. To feel as if he wiped away the pain. But some things you just can't wipe away.

The bathroom was a mess. Piss was everywhere. Cocaine under the toilet seat.

He sighs; moving things was a no, wiping it down on the other hand was a yes.

'She needs rehab,' he thinks to himself while scrubbing the sink.

The burning scent of bleach cloaked the other mysterious scents. By the time he finishes cleaning the living room, it's about time to make lunch. He throws away his gloves and scrubs his arms and hands raw.

Marylin stands in the doorway, staring.

"You cleaned?" She asks her voice to be deeper and sharper than before.

"You sobered up?" he counters.

"With the promise of food? Yes," she takes a seat at the table.

Her hands run off the surface, and she sighs.

"Yes?" Tor asks, pulling a fresh pot from the dish rack.

"Sorry you had to see me like that, baby boy. You know I'm trying to get clean," Marylin says.

"From what? The heroin? The cocaine? The alcohol? The cigarettes?" he scoffs, that wasn't even the full list.

She still had plenty of things she needed to get rid of. "All of it, baby. I know it's messing me up."

He looks back at her.

She was slumped in her chair, her hair a fro of matted curls. Her eyes were drooping, and she kept touching stuff. She was probably having a fit of some sort.

"I'll be done in a bit. Why don't you set the table, hmm?"

She stands up and joins him at the counters.

"While you're at it, take a shower." She glares at him, but it's soft and threat-less.

"Okay, Dad." She mocks.

He snickers and cracks open a few eggs. Tor keeps checking in the fridge for something...anything, really.

"I'm going grocery shopping. Not just gonna eat eggs." Tor mumbles.

Marylin puts her small, warm hand over his. He eyes it before meeting her gaze.

"What's troubling you?" he shrugs, closing the fridge.

"You only got eggs," Tor says.

"*Tor. Lue. Bac.* That is not the problem."

He takes his hand from under hers and brings both of her hands into his.

"I left someone in a pretty upsetting situation." Marylin waits for more. Tor kisses her hands.

"Go wash," Tor says.

Marylin pouts but leaves to do what her son said.

He sets the table and finishes their eggs and cheese sandwiches.

Tor types shopping into the calendar for later today.

"Tor." His mom calls from the front of the house. He jogs over to her, approving of the towel over her neck and her changed clothes.

"Is that yours?" She asks with wide eyes.

She points outside to the white Volvo parked in front of her house.

"Yes. Like it?" She nods, opening the door and squints at it." You can take me grocery shopping then." Tor says.

She raises her brows at him.

"Really? I can't though...need to renew my license." Marylin says with a sigh.

Tor shrugs, pulling her inside the house. He closes and locks the door. Checking twice to be sure.

"This yours?" She asks, pulling his suitcase deeper down the hallway.

"Yes." He answers. She takes it and drops it by the first door, his old room.

"Why's it in the hall?" she asks. Her voice fades through the hall as she dips into his room and back out. He shrugs, though she can't see him and sits at the table. Marylin joins him eagerly, snatching up her sandwich.

"Forgot I had bread." She chokes out.

He shakes his head and eats his food much more slowly. Tor cleans their plates when they finish.

"Why'd you come home, Tor?" Marylin asks. They move the conversation to the living room. Her *stuff* had been placed under the table, and the area was sparkling like when he was a child.

"I missed you."

She flips him the finger. "Liar. You get that from your dad."

She scratches at her neck and stops looking at the coffee table.

"To get you some help," Tor says honestly.

Marylin raises a brow at her youngest. "Nah, I'm doing fine." She says.

Tor glares and sinks into the cushion. "No, you're not. You need help, but I can only get it to you if you are willing to take it."

"You want me in rehab? I'd rather go rot in an old folks home." Marylin spits.

"You will. After rehab," he laughs and stops because of the look on her face.

"I'm kidding, Mom. You own this house; no one is sending you anywhere."

She puts her head on the cushion.

"That's not true." She mumbles.

Tor forces the frown from his lips.

Chapter Four

Tor stares dumbfounded at his mother.

"What do you mean it's not true?" She shrugs.

"Marilyn." He says.

She sighs exasperatedly.

He inclines his head, and she shrugs again. "Mom, please."

She stands and grabs some of the mail he brought in. "I owe the bank some money for the water and electricity."

Tor takes the mail and opens it. His eyes sweep the list of due and paid. The outrageous number at the bottom. He pinches the bridge of his nose and sighs.

"Why haven't you paid?" he asks. She plops down and works the tension out of her feet. "Why—"

"I was busy." She cuts in. Tor looks down at the number and the QR code. He takes out his phone, scans it, and pays.

"I don't care anymore. Let's go."

"To pay the bill? Tor, baby, I don't have the money." Marylin says softly.

It reminds him of the voice she used to use when he asked for field trip money or lunch money.

"Took care of it. We're going grocery shopping." Marylin gets back up, mimicking his dropped shoulders.

"I see. Thank you, baby boy."

"I can't have you losing the only place you're welcome." He throws the paper down and heads towards the door.

"Put on your coat, meet me in the car." He calls, throwing on his shoes and his coat.

The pathway was worse than he thought. The walk to the car was slick with ice.

His stomach turns at the thought of his mother slipping. He pulls his phone out and types in a bag of salt and a shovel into a memo.

His mother makes it out unscathed and ogles the interior of his car.

"Leather seats that warm themselves? What else you got, an ice cream dispenser?" She asks.

"No."

Marylin frowns at his curt tone. She wrings her hands in her lap and stares out the window.

They pass Juice, standing on the side of the road.

He raises his fist in greeting. Tor raises his own.

They step out of the car at the department store and grab a cart. The walk around the store is slow and tiring. Lifting and checking fruits and vegetables. Weighing slabs of freshly cut meat. Pricing breads and dairy products. And finally, some spice, a large bag of salt, and a shovel.

Tor keeps his eyes on each person, watching, waiting for someone to recognize him. Hoping they don't.

The trip back was a lot louder with his mother singing her midday gospel.

Tor pulls the car up behind another. His stomach drops to his feet when he gets out.

The man by the car turns around and smiles sweetly. Sickly sweet.

"Mom, grab the milk and go inside." She looks between the two of them.

"Friend of yours?"

"Yes."

She looks between them again with a frown. "Alright. Come in quick or the groceries will freeze."

"Yes, ma'am."

She takes the bags with the dairy into the house. Tor closes the distance between him and his *friend*.

"Sir," Tor says.

"You must have heard what happened. Since you and the rest went into hiding...You know, it was hard to find you. Good thing Sullivan knew where you went, or I'd be lost." The man says slowly, pronouncing each word. His thick Spanish accent makes it sound menacing.

"Great." Tor deadpans.

The fact the two were talking at all meant the gangs were getting closer to an all out war. That *he* would have to pick a side. Everyone would know he was a trader, double agent, disloyal and nothing breaks trust like disloyalty.

Palo pops a cigarette into his mouth. He flicks his lighter open and covers it from the wind.

"You have something you want from me?" Tor asks. His hands flinch at Palo's every move. At any moment he might need to defend himself.

"How was it going?" Palo asks.

"Fine. Doing what I needed, but never more than I could fix." Tor says, stuffing his hands into his pockets.

But he wasn't was he? He was clearly more loyal to the South Sanz, and if Palo had any inkling, he was hiding it well. Tor's stomach flips as Palo inches closer. He inches back.

"So, what about the explosion? Sources told me that you checked in." Palo says, leveling his eyes on Tor.

"*Everyone* checked in. But not everyone stayed. What about you? It was mandatory."

"The boss's birthday is not a mandatory event for more...*respectable members*," Palo says.

Tor shrugs and stuffs his hands into his pockets. Feigning a calm demeanor. His heart raced, his blood warming him, despite the bitter cold.

"The Vipers are having a meeting here at the strip club. You should know which one, bring your badge, and we'll talk about our next moves," Palo pauses. "Unless you'd rather get de-initiated? I heard you were sweet on one of the Sanz girls." Palo says. His eyes lower to Tor's chain.

Tor scoffs. "What's that supposed to mean?" He asks.

His heart sank. *Did he know about Jaamini?*

Palo drops his cigarette, blowing the smoke into Tor's face and steps through it.

"It means you have reason to be unloyal. I won't stand for that as the new leader."

Tor holds his breath, turning away from Palo, just an excuse to put more distance between them. "I'm still loyal to the Vipers. One explosion doesn't mean a thing."

Palo pats his face and grins. The sour trail of smoke engulfing them.

"Good." Palo steps back to the door of his car. "You go take care of that good woman. Don't want you dying prematurely, *do we*?" He gets in without waiting for an answer and pulls away.

Tor watches until his car disappears down the road.

Then he breathes in deeply.

"Pop the trunk!" Juice calls.

Tor's face scrunches up, and he turns around. "What?"

"Yous gon' make that little old lady bring in the groceries?"

Tor shakes his head and pops the trunk.

The two of them bring all the bags and lock up.

"You want dinner, don't you?" Tor asks while they put away the food.

"Why else would I help?" Juice says.

"Mad disingenuous," Tor says under his breath.

"What does that mean?" Juice asks, holding a box of mac and cheese.

Tor keeps his mouth shut and stacks the cans. Marylin joins them with a tea kettle, setting it on the stove.

"Who was that man, Tor?" Marylin asks.

"A friend."

"He didn't sound like a friend," she says. She puts her hands on her hips and stares her son down.

"Don't worry about it, ma."

She sighs and starts fiddling with the latch on the pot.

"I want you to be safe. No amount of money is worth losing your life over."

Tor finishes cleaning up all the bags.

"I know."

She hums and grabs Juice by the ear.

"And what are you doing here, you little thief? Thought I forgot? Where's my good china?"

"*Man*, I ain't got no china!" Juice yells and pulls away. He grabs another box from the bags.

The three of them put away the rest of the food and sat down with a steaming cup of tea.

"Mama, you trust me, right?" Tor asks quietly.

Juice looks between the two of them, and Marylin sighs.

"To an extent. Make your point."

"We can talk about it later." He says, sipping gingerly at the burning liquid. When he finishes his cup, he fastens his coat and takes Juice out to the front.

"Put down the salt." He says over the rushing wind.

Juice sucks his teeth, puts them open, and starts tossing salt.

Tor takes the shovel and moves as much of the soft snow as he can, and avoids all the ice for Juice to throw salt on.

By the time they had cleared most of the path, the streetlights had come on, and their noses were running. The two, while hot from movement were still shivering in their thick coats.

"Can...we just stop?" Juice complains. He looked more sober now than in the past three years Tor had known him.

"Yeah, come in and warm up. I'll make dinner."

They unbundled in the foyer, and Tor left Juice to sit and warm up on the couch. Tor briefly looks around for his mother but doesn't see her.

Instead, he takes out the pans from earlier and starts cooking chicken and fries. It was strange being back here. It was strange to cook again in this home; without the presence of his mother, it felt like a whole different house. When he was little, Marylin always cooked with him, taught him that knowing how to take care of himself would be his greatest skill.

Halfway through frying the chicken, his mother stumbles in with a glass in her hand.

She smiles, placing down the half glass of wine.

"Not drunk," she slurs a bit.

Tor rolls his eyes, taking the cup and placing it high in the cabinet where she could not reach. She punches his arm and sits down at the table.

"Why?" she yells out and rests her head on the table. Seconds later, she's snoring loudly. Probably not from the wine, he had to have found something else during her absence.

Tor calls Juice in and tells him to finish the wine.

"You's mama gonna hate me." He says after taking a huge gulp.

"You don't care, and neither do I. Grab a plate."

Juice complies, grabbing the three of them. Tor shakes his mother awake, and she takes tiny bites with her eyes half closed. He knew a downer when he saw one.

Tor quietly rages. 'What could she be thinking?'

Why was she like this? Was it his fault, was his father's fault? Or did the blame really fall on her?

"You tryna get her clean or something?" Juice asks. He swirls the red wine in its glass.

Tor sighs deeply, he unfurls his hands on the table.

"Yeah. Can't have her dying because of liver failure or overdose."

Juice shrugs. "She gon be alright. She's been a fighter since she was a kid."

Tor makes a face.

Childhood was a sore subject. He still didn't want to remember anything from growing up in the boring town, poorer than the tourists swept in by the sea.

Juice puts Marylin's food away and helps put her back in her bed.

"Can't believe she gave up hot chicken for sleep." He says, closing the door.

"Thanks for your help, man."

"Yous know I got you. Come by the club, man."

"I'm heading to bed. I'll be there tomorrow." Tor says.

Juice sighs.

"Alright. Peace."

"Peace."

Tor locks the door, then shuts and locks the window. He pulls down the blinds and cleans the kitchen table again.

When there was nothing to clean, he stood in front of his old bedroom door.

Swallowing down the discomfort, he steps into the room and turns on the light.

Dust had settled on every surface. A mildew, musky scent wafts from the ground and the bed. The window had frost covering it and was blocked by one of the bushes outside. From his window, he could barely see the street.

Tor sighs instantly, regretting it. Choked by the dirt, he coughs until he has to exit the room.

"She doesn't clean shit. Some homecoming."

Tor cleans the room with a clothespin on his nose until the air is breathable. He cracks open the window with some effort and lets in the bitter cold. The mildew scent clings to the sheets, despite the Febreze he sprays.

Against the odds, he manages to fall asleep curled up on his coat on the floor.

Chapter Five

IN THE MORNING, TOR takes his mother to her doctor's appointment. He sits inside, waiting for the doctor.

"You shoulda stayed out there," Marylin mumbles, yawning into her hand.

"No, for what. Curiosity would have killed me," Tor says.

"You don't need to know about my body."

He chuckles.

Tor sits up straighter when the doctor knocks.

"Come in." His mother mumbles.

The doctor enters and clicks the door shut. She smiles at Marylin and halts when she sees Tor.

"Oh, what a surprise." The woman says.

Tor smiles. "Hey, Lemon."

"It's Doctor Teller now."

"I can see that...Doctor Teller." He says with a smirk.

The doctor places down her clipboard and turns on the sink. She gives her hands a good scrub and dries them before turning back to the dio.

"Alright, Marylin, what do we have you in here for today?" she asks, pulling her rolling chair over to sit in front of them.

"Check-up," Marilyn says with a yawn.

They go through the standard check of her eyes, ears, heart and weight. Once they were done, Tor was asked to leave the room for a minute. He sighs and grabs his coat. Outside the room, many nurses whiz by him, and doctors pass tools to each other or speak slowly to children.

One of the doctors stopped in front of him.

"Hey Tor! Do you remember me?" The man says, straightening up, his white coat clings tightly to his sides and his arms bulge in the sleeves.

'Someone's been hitting the gym.'

"Uh, not exactly," Tor says. The older man chuckles and nods.

"I delivered you and treated your sprained ankle when you were a kid."

Tor frowns. The older man scratched at the back of his neck and smiled honestly.

"Oh, well, thanks, man," Tor says.

"You're welcome." The doctor turns away and starts down the hall.

"Doc!" Tor calls.

The man turns around with raised brows.

"Got a question... It's private." The two of them step out of the hall into his office.

"What is it, my boy?" He asks, sitting on the edge of the desk. The wood creaked under his weight.

"Do you know about any good rehabs?" Tor asks, swallowing dryly. Despair creeps up his chest. Closing in from his heart, squeezing his throat.

His eye flits around the room, landing on his nameplate.

Doctor Gray hums and looks around his office as well. He passes Tor and opens the top cabinet of his files, flipping through until he pulls out a manila folder.

"Yes, here we are." He passes over three sheets of paper and two brochures.

"It's for your mom, right? You're a good son. I saw your eldest brother recently...he wasn't as nice."

"I don't care much about them...thank you, Doctor. I won't forget this." Tor says.

"They're expensive." Doctor Gray says, closing up the filing cabinet.

Tor briefly looks over the papers and then nods.

"I'll figure it out." Doctor Gray remains silent for a while.

"Good luck, Tor."

Tor nods, thanks him, before excusing himself to the hallway.

Doctor Teller pops into the hallway and looks around before waving him over. She eyes his stash of papers but doesn't ask. She ushered him into the room and sat him down.

Marylin smacks her lips on some candy in her hand.

"Your mother has just informed me she hasn't told you, but she has very high cholesterol. She needs to start taking her medication. I have also prescribed her some vitamin tablets that she needs to start taking." She turns away from Tor and levels her eyes at his mother.

"And *you* need to stop drinking, even if it's wine. You need to be clean and take your meds. Your health is important, Miss. Marylin."

Marylin nods, stands up, and shoulders her purse. "I hear you." She says calmly and pulls on her coat.

Tor waves goodbye to Doctor Teller. She puts his mother's prescription in his hand.

"I hope you make the right choice." She says and nods her head at his papers.

"You know me, Lemon, I always make the right choice."

She hums and lets him leave the room first.

Tor takes his mother home and heads down to the strip club.

The small, decrepit brick building had probably been here longer than he had been born. But the second floor was recently added, and it was an obviously hideous attachment with bright red, clean bricks that had no moss or piss stains.

Tor parks his car, causing a few staggering men to look his way and eye him. He straightens out his trench coat and pops the collar around his neck.

The chilly morning air almost caught him off guard. He should have known when he woke up as an icicle, that it was going to be cold.

His shades fog up when he breathes, and his cold chain makes him flinch as it brushes against his skin.

The door to the strip club was barred and locked, as he expected. He walks around the back and raises his hand to the door. He gives one look to both sides before knocking four times in succession, then waits a few seconds before repeating the sequence and adding a knock with his other hand to complete the secret knock.

Locks unclick and slide out of place before the door swings open. Juice smirks at Tor before stepping out of the way.

"Listen, man, you're fam, but um...you're early for openin. There's a few dancers around, if you're looking for a private session." He says.

Tor shakes his head and blows into his hand rubbing them together.

"It's fine, Juice. I came for a meeting."

Juice raises his brows and nods at him. "Oh that."

"They are in the boss's room. You still remember where that's at, right?"

Tor nods and walks through the back to the office by the private dance rooms. He thinks it's a very interesting place to have an office.

A few women walk by smelling heavily of fruits, one winks at him. Another stops him, "Tor!"

Her shinny pumps, match the greasy glittering floor.

He stops walking to the back, the dim lights reflect of her glitter filled make up.

"Oh, hey," he says. He doesn't remember her at all.

"It's me, Messy Vicky."

He nods. "Ah, hey how are you?"

She smiles a wide, and crooked smile. "So much better now. Came for a dance?" she asks wiggling her brows.

He quickly steps away. "Uh no, but thank you. Maybe I'll check back in later."

She smiles. "It's been too long love, stop by soon okay."

The other girls wrap her arm in theirs and they walk off giggling.

Their perfume lingers in the air, and on his coat where she touched him. Tor wipes the area off hoping it doesn't cling for long.

When he entered the room, all eyes shifted to him. One of the members puts out his cigar and glares.

The walls are yellowing from the smoke, the room chalk full of metal fold out chairs and very bored looking people.

A familiar couple smiles at him and waves him over. He closes the door behind him and enters the room. Tor passed a few miscellaneous members that he could just barely remember.

He takes a seat by Luca, probably the best person here if he were being honest.

"Glad you made it out, kiddo," Luca says softly. The older Italian man leans lightly on his cobra-head staff. The ruby eyes glint up at him in the dark light of the room.

"Glad you made it too."

The two men nod to each other before sliding their attention to the front of the room.

Sat behind the desk was Palo, who flexes his fingers and leans forward.

"Tor, *the mole*. Welcome to our first meeting as the new age of Vipers." Tor takes a sweep of the room. A girl his age smiles at him.

He inclines his head and sums up the last few people of the Vipers.

'No one important.'

He was an efficient mole, it seemed. Maybe too efficient.

"It has come to our attention that you haven't reported anything in a while. So, tell us. Where are the Sanz hiding?" Tor furrows his brows and clears his throat.

"I don't know. Haven't been there in a minute. You know how fast-paced our lifestyle is." Palo blinks at him and rubs a hand over his bald head.

His hands were tattooed down to the fingertips, just like Tor's, but his looked venomous, spelling out his name and an acronym Tor knew nothing about.

"You don't know where they're hiding? And you had no idea about the explosion?" Tor opens his mouth to explain, but there's nothing to say.

He didn't know...that it would be such a big explosion.

"Right."

Palo stands and crosses the room. His many years giving tattoos had worn down his back, causing him to hunch while he walked.

Yet, the whole crowd began to part like a mass, a sea. A few of them twitched instinctively towards their weapons, to protect themselves, to respond to an order. He wasn't sure, and didn't want to find out.

Tor sat up straighter until the man stood just above him.

"What *do you have* to report to us?" His breath caused the air to warm.

The smell of cigarettes and cigars makes Tor internally gag.

"I—" Tor starts but stops himself. Sweat forms at his hairline, and his ear grow warm.

He had to think of something, their drug drop locations, their night walking locations, anything really.

But with all the time he'd spent with them, the most he really knew was that they did all their illegal business to keep others off the streets.

It was strange, we're they even a real gang?

They owned laundromats, restaurants, warehouses that housed imported goods, casinos, clubs, wineries and real estate, they only had a few routine blocks where they took in anyone who'd started dealing or pimping and turned them into something more, something better.

How could he betray that? They were his family after all.

"Never mind Tor, you are obviously quite useless when it comes to retaining information. That's too bad. You seem so good with your mother. It would be terrible if you just...forgot about her."

Tor grits his teeth and glares at the large form of Palo's back.

Palo takes a seat behind the desk.

"That's very okay. I have something for you to do anyway. *If* you want to keep living willie nillie and taking care of your mother." Palo says.

Tor releases his fists and lays his hands flat against his thighs.

Resolve building from his anger, Tor steadies himself.

"What is it, Sir?" Tor asks.

A smile stretches across Palo's face. His dark eyes gleam just like the rubies in Luca's cane. He leans in like a predator baiting its prey.

Tor holds his gaze.

Chapter Six

Tor takes the first step in front of the all-black building.

Pretty sleek for a precinct.

He wipes sweaty palms on his jeans and leaves his hands hanging by his side so they can be seen at all times. He didn't want any *accidents*.

Stepping into the building, the humid air hits him.

A few cops sit behind desks, clicking away. Some phones ring on and off.

People sit in a row of chairs against the wall, down a very long hallway. On the left, he can see the door leading to the cells.

"Can I help you?" A petite woman calls from behind the desk. Her light blonde hair is pulled into a low bun at the nape of her neck. Boney fingers stretch fast across the keyboard while she stares dead-eyed into his face. He steps up to the counter and clears his throat.

He leans in and speaks lowly to keep the conversation between the two of them.

"I had a quick question."

"Yes?" She asks her nails to halt above the Q and R keys. He looks away quickly.

"Is there a number for anonymous tips?"

The woman's hands lower to the base of her keyboard, and she raises a brow.

A low hum rumbles from her throat as she pulls an index card from a stack and pops the top off a ballpoint pen.

She lowers her eyes at him once more, taking in his long coat. Form-fitting pants and tucked-in button-up. She approves with her eyes and scrawls out a few notes and a set of numbers on the card before sliding it over to him.

"That should do the trick." She says loud enough for all to hear.

A man walks by from the corner of the room, glances at them, only to turn away and head back down the hall.

Tor watches his retreating before taking the card and slipping it into his inside pocket.

"Thank you."

"Thank you in advance, sir." He nods and steps away.

Tor gave one last glance to the young men sitting in uncomfortable positions, wearing matching sets of cuffs.

He shakes his head and sets back into the morning's salty air. He could almost taste the ocean over the buildings, and he could see the large ships and a few smaller boats docking at the harbor.

He doesn't take out the index card until he is secured in his car with the doors locked. A number for anonymous tips, along with instructions on how to submit a tip anonymously and without being questioned. Prevention hotlincs.

At the very bottom was a familiar set of digits, he smirked.

'Still got it, I see.' He thinks of stashing away the index card and ignoring the woman's number. His...whatever Jaamini was to him right now, wouldn't appreciate him taking this woman's phone number and saving it.

He pulls out of the parking lot, looking back at it in his rearview mirror. His hand finds the volume button on the steering wheel, and he turns his music up.

Old school '90s rap filters through the speakers.

This time he made it out of there, next time he sees a precinct might be the last time he sees the outside world.

If only they knew.

Marylin slaps her son's hand away when he helps her out of the car.

He smiles at her glare, and they walk to the back of the car to the open trunk.

"I'm telling you I checked it out thoroughly," Tor says firmly.

His mother makes another face before pulling her duffel bag from the trunk.

He grabs her matching suitcase. "Listen, Ma, would I ever do you wrong?"

"Where'd you get the money?" She counters.

Her hardened brown eyes had seen and experienced a lot, but never had they held so much disbelief and doubt aimed towards him.

In the sunlight's warm embrace, he could see how much he looked like her, at the same time, he had his father's build and blue eyes.

Tor clears his throat and takes the bag gently from her shoulder. Relieving her of the weight.

"You know, ma," he says softly. He had grown tired of her blatant disregard for his aid. He wants to do right by her, but *she couldn't see that, could she?*

"I don't know shit." She says, folding her arms together.

Tor closes the trunk to keep the light trickle of snow from falling into it.

"You don't have anything to say?"

Tor sighs and rolls his shoulders.

"You said you'd check in. You said you'd try." Tor says.

"I have a right to know what kinda money you're checking me in with," she hisses, moving closer as others make their way through the parking lot with their family.

"It's clean, Marylin," Tor says. He moves around her.

He was hurt; that much was obvious. But what he was doing with his time was no better than what she was doing with hers.

Marylin follows her son, her heeled boots clicking against the asphalt in tune with his Timberlands.

The two amble into the building and give it a good once-over.

Tor tries to ignore how boring it looks.

"Mom will be well taken care of." He says under his breath. He needed some reassurance, and the weeping older man in front of him was no help.

The man was wearing clean clothes, but his frail gray hair gave a looking glass into his life, his struggle with addiction. But the worst part was his wild eyes that said it all.

"You want me in here with him?" His mom asks mockingly. She jabs her thumb in his direction.

Tor ignores her biting comment and shuffles around them to the front desk. The lady stands up quickly and moves around the desk, her scrubs swishing as she walks.

"Miss Marylin." The lady says. Her name tag shines from the light overhead, blocking the edge of her name. Tor didn't bother to try reading it either.

"Yes?" His mother asks, looking wide-eyed between the nurse and Tor.

"We'll show you to your room now."

His mother nods absently.

Tor inclines his head after the nurse and follows her. His mother wrings her hands and sighs before joining them down the winding hall to the room at the end.

"Your room has a view of the sea. Your son says you *love* the sea."

His mother doesn't say anything, lingering in the doorway of the room. She gazes at the bed against the wall close to the window. Its bedspread was white. The end table on its side was white, and the vase on top of it held white lilies.

Marylin frowns.

Tor makes note of her unease and places her bag on the bed. He unzips it and reaches straight to the bottom for the gifts he'd packed.

He puts the picture frames down on her end table and stuffs three lavender stalks into the vase. He switches the pillow case out with a silk one to protect her hair. Lastly, he fishes around and pulls out a stack of books tied by a yellow ribbon. He takes a *ta-da* stance, arms outstretched with a wide smile on his face.

Marylin's shoulders drop and she grins. She enters the room and walks around the nurse, setting up, to throw her arms around her son. She hugs him as tight as she can.

He hugs his mother's smaller frame, letting his mind take him back to his childhood, just for a moment.

Warm cookies and smooth jazz. His mother dances around the room singing his favorite song. He could feel the warmth in her deep voice even then, when he hugged her tightly.

Those were different times.

The nurse steps to the door.

"I will give you a few minutes. Take your time." She says and walks away quietly.

Marylin lets go of her son and unties the books. She flips through the stack, nodding at some and raising her brows at others. He smiles.

"Oh." Marylin folds her arms over her chest and plops down on the edge of the bed. "I haven't forgotten. I'm still mad at you."

Tor sighs and takes a seat next to his mom. He moves her bag further towards the center of the bed and places his hands on hers.

"Mom, I had to do this like this. You need this help *now*, not in forty years or however long it would take me to get this kind of money." Marylin pulls her hands from his and grabs his face instead.

Her warm hands instantly bring him back to a better time. He could see it just behind his eyelids.

"Tor, you know I love you no matter what. Just like with all my kids." She says. She makes sure he is looking into her eyes before continuing. "I want you to know that I don't blame you for this life. I don't blame you for not finishing school, I don't blame you for the others' leaving. I don't blame you for your father."

Tor sucks in a breath, standing up straighter.

"Those things were out of your control, and a lot of it was my fault..." She chuckles. "All of it was my fault. But baby boy, after this. When I get out, I want you to promise you'll stop."

Tor looks down at the tattoo on the back of his hand. Roses and lavender, his mother's favorites. The chain that swung on his neck, his mother's gift to him.

He swallows.

"I promise." He says, placing his forehead on hers.

"You know, once you're in that life...well, birds of a feather flock together. Don't let them brand your wings, baby."

He chuckles.

'Did I get my weird quote habit from mom? Probably.'

"I won't, Mama. Now settle in. I'll come to see you as soon as possible."

"Where are you going?" she asks.

"If I'm going to leave, I need to finish a few things first."

His mother gives him another big hug and a kiss. Then she starts unpacking her bags.

Tor blows a kiss at her, though she isn't looking, and darts out of the building and back into his car.

He whips out his phone and rustles around his coat pocket until he finds the large white index card.

'It's time.'

Chapter Seven

IT TAKES A FEW days before anything happens. And those few days chip away at Tor bit by bit.

The tick of his watch drives him insane in the silence of the house.

The cold creeps in through the walls, seeping into the air, the floor, the furniture.

Tor stands up.

The news plays on the TV behind him. He watches another group of South Sanz members get hauled into the back of police vans.

Inside, he was aching more than when he had to cover for his...*for Jaamini* planting bombs in the casino. Things still felt fuzzy from that day, surreal even.

The only thing he really remembered was running and getting into his car, and then the blast. The airbags popped out of the wheel and smacked a tree.

Whatever else happened when the building dropped, he wasn't conscious for.

Tor takes a seat and stretches his arms. He needed to focus on something. His stomach was already rolling at the thought of speaking to Palo, knowing that he's held up his end of the bargain.

His phone starts to ring, and he checks the caller ID before answering. *Palo.*

'Speak of the devil, and he shall appear.'

He clears his throat and answers the call.

"Hello, sir." Palo chuckles coldly.

"Open the door," Palo says and hangs up.

Tor stares down at his phone for a moment before craning his neck to look towards the front door.

He gulps inaudibly and tucks his gun into his waistband.

His steps thud against the floor in rhythm with his heartbeat.

Tor takes a deep breath and unlocks the door. When it opens Palo barrels past him, brushing roughly against his shoulder.

Tor looks around the street, noting every little detail he can. One streetlight. Three cars on the left, two on the right, with no snow on them, exhausts running.

'Palo didn't come alone.'

He closes the front door and locks it.

He had three bullets left in his gun. Hopefully, he wouldn't need it.

Palo paces back and forth in front of the couch, staring dead at the TV.

"What the hell is this?" Palo asks, turning to Tor.

Tor stops in the hallway.

"What is what?" Tor asks, already knowing what he was about to say.

Palo points at the screen and rounds the couch to stand in front of Tor.

"Listen, boy, you need to do more to prove your reliability."

"Yes, sir."

"Don't—Yes, sir, me, *tu idoita*!" Palo huffs out a deep breath; a red flush covers his face and ears. It even stretches down his neck to the collar of his shirt.

Palo closes the distance between them, pointing a finger at Tor. Under his nails is a thin layer of dirt and what looks to be blood. The scent of cigarettes blends with a musky aroma and a hint of coffee.

Tor holds his breath, turning his head to the side.

"Once we have cleared the riffraff from the streets, we're going to move in on them from the core. I mean, *war* boy, war like no other. I won't stop until every single last one of them is dead. Do you hear me? Dead." Palo shouts.

Tor nods.

"How...exactly are we going to do that? I mean, they have hundreds more people than we do," Tor says meekly.

Palo chuckles. His hot breath wafts into Tor's nose.

Tor backs away slightly, his stomach starting to cramp up.

"Well, first we set them up. Then, we tip off the cops. Once the main heads are distracted," He slaps his hands together, making Tor jump.

Tor's skin crawled at just the thought.

"We strike." Palo finishes. His dull brown eyes sparkled for the first time since Tor had meant him.

"Great...one question," Tor interjects. Palo looks away from his hands and up at Tor, who is a head taller.

Even though Palo typically wore shoes that leveled their heights.

The older Spanish man raises a brow and leans forward.

"You want everyone dead? Including your nieces and nephews? Your brother and your sister-in-law? *Everyone*?" Tor asks.

From the look in Palo's eyes, he could guess the answer without it being said. Palo raises a hand to stop him from talking.

"Listen, boy, and listen well. They ain't no *familia*. Their lying, scheming, traitors who kill anyone for their gain." Palo nods and steps out of Tor's personal space. "You wouldn't understand," Palo says.

Tor flexes his hands, keeping them close to his holster.

"Try me," Tor says, standing up straighter.

Palo pops the collar of his shirt and stuffs his hands into his pockets.

"Twelve years ago, the South Sanz fell apart. Their friend, comrade, and my brother Sergio was killed. On that night, Sullivan ran away from the gang, never to be seen again, and with him went his son and his wife. Everyone else was locked up, killed, or lost without or sense of direction. And with no one to lead, the South Sanz fell to shit. We all felt the loss of young Sergio. And now it's time to get revenge for all the good blood that's been spilled." Palo says.

Tor relaxes his hands, letting them fall limply by his waist.

"My condolences, but if you don't mind me asking, who killed him?"

"His twin. Sullivan Sanz." Palo says venomously.

Tor frowns. He pinches the bridge of his nose and tries to wrap his head around the situation. *One twin kills the other, goes into hiding for a decade, then comes back, reignites the gang and then tries to massacre the other gang?*

Palo looks at Tor.

"Forget it, new blood. There's nothing you can do about this age-old rivalry anyway. Just keep getting the weak ones locked away." Palo closes in again, his brown eyes burning with one of life's deadliest sins, wrath. "While you're at it, prepare for war."

Palo walks around him briskly and to the door. He stops in front of it with his hand on the knob.

"And Tor?" Palo calls.

"Yes, sir?"

"If I find out you are holding back information, you can forget about seeing your mom again."

Tor's hands ball into fists, and he watches Palo disappear into the street in his black car.

Five other cars disengage from their parking spots and follow behind him.

Tor waits until he can't see them anymore to close and lock his door.

He fishes for his phone in his pocket and starts making calls. His throat goes dry at the end of the hour, his numerous calls starting to wear him down.

Tor steps into the kitchen and grabs himself some water. From the window, he could see out into the backyard.

The sounds of children yelling softly play in his mind. He could see the numerous brown children running around the scraggly backyard with bright orange and blue water guns.

One of the kids falls and starts crying. The youngest and the weakest. The other kids gather around laughing and shoot him with their water guns until they run dry. Then they run inside, together, like a pack of wolves out for blood.

Tor shakes the memory from the forefront of his head. What would he tell them in the afterlife?

'I tried to save her.'

They wouldn't listen even if they saw it with their own eyes.

It would always be his fault, wouldn't it?

Tor opens his phone and scrolls through until he finds her contact. He clicks the button and presses the phone to his ear.

"Hello," Jaamini answers softly.

"Hey, love," Tor starts. "I promised I'd be coming back."

Jaamini is silent on the phone. "Well, you know where I am."

Tor smiles though she can't see. "Wait for me, I'm on my way to you."

How many lies until he became a liar? At least this time he meant it. He owed it to her, he owed it to them to wrap this all up with a bow, and never open it again.

Chapter Eight

It wasn't exactly a problem for Tor that he was headed back into the police station at eight am. He had business here after all.

The real problem was the fact that a few of the officers were beginning to recognize his face. They watch him curiously as he passes by.

His hands shake in his pockets. Maybe just maybe, this would be his last time as a free man.

It only took one small movement, a strange look, or a weird string of sentences; and everything he's knows would come crashing down around him.

Tor stopped at the information desk and looked around at the people sitting in the waiting area.

"Hello, sir, can I help you?" The woman asks. Tor looks away from the people, and he hands the lady a piece of paper.

She looks down at the series of numbers and back up at him.

"Sorry, sir, but I can't take your number," she says lightly, but she smiles through it.

The blonde twists a few strands of her hair behind her ear where her low ponytail sat.

"Send that to the Chief," Tor says as calmly as possible before walking out.

She stares, stunned at the front door before looking at the digits more closely. It wasn't a phone number.

She bolts up and to the Chief of Police's office.

Tor shakes off the feeling of being watched and climbs into his car. After all of this, he would need a drink.

His hands shake when he drives, and his eyes check his mirrors over and over.

He pulls into an alley and waits until a red Toyota pulls in behind him. He sighs in relief at the car and pops the door open.

Tor waits until the familiar bob of purple pops over the shell of the door.

He gets out and smiles at her.

Sey walks up to him.

"Missed me?" She asks. Sey is his friend, a member of the South Sanz, and probably the nicest woman he's ever met who works the streets at night.

"Yeah, a little. How's everyone?" he asks, pulling her into a tight hug.

"Fine. Lots of newbies are going missing. Some of our walkers, too."

She didn't know the half of it. What was to come next, this was only the surface of the pain he'd be causing them. His family, his friends.

Tor frowns. Even Sey got put in danger. He could just feel the disappointment rolling off of her.

"You know why I'm doing it," Tor complains.

"Doesn't make it any less painful, Tor."

"I know. *Lo siento.*" Tor says.

Sey shrugs her shoulders and looks down at the leather seats in his car.

The little asian woman could probably fit in his pocket, but that spitfire was scary on the field, and didn't need any help.

"Sorry isn't going to cut it. Unless you and the boss have some sort of plan to get all my girls out of the pen by Friday night, then I'm going to be one hell of a problem for the two of you."

Tor holds his hands up in surrender.

"Guess we better get a move on then..." Tor's voice trails off when he sees a sleek black Corvette roll into the alleyway, locking them in from that side.

"Speak of the devil-" Sey mumbles.

"And he shall appear." Tor finishes.

Tor and Sey stand guard, hoping that Sullivan is in a good mood today.

Black, glossy Oxfords show under the Falcon Wing doors. Sullivan steps out and straightens his three-piece, blood-red suit. The low stream of light behind him caused his silhouette to glow brightly.

Tor tries to swallow past his dry throat.

Sullivan tilts his head at the two of them before closing his doors and walking over.

His Oxfords crunch against the gravel, the pants of his suit leave a soft swish, and the light catches on his Grandmaster Chime; the gold-encrusted face of the watch radiates the light bouncing on it. The small clocks tick soundlessly.

Tor shudders at the dough Sullivan no doubt forked over during the purchase of such a piece. Had to have been millions.

Tor stands impossibly straighter when Sullivan enters their personal space. Sullivan's dark brown eyes sweep between the two. He scratches lightly at his beard before stuffing his hands into his suit pockets.

"Hey, boss man," Sey utters.

He locks eyes with her and nods.

"You have information for me, don't you?" He asks Tor.

Tor thinks before a light bulb goes off in his head.

"Oh yeah, it's Palo. He...well, he wants you dead, and he plans to kill you himself." As the words leave Tor's mouth, he wishes the world would split below him and swallow him whole.

Sullivan remains quiet before a light smirk graces his face. His smiling was a blood-cooling sight.

"I see. I'll take care of him." Sullivan checks the time on his watch.

"Bring together the Vipers at your *hideout*." He gives Tor a once-over. "Come prepared, boy."

Tor salutes Sullivan and waits with bated breath for him to leave.

Sullivan turns his attention to Sey.

"You have a new assignment."

Sey frowns and shakes her head lightly. A fruity scent wafts from her hair.

Did they all smell like that?

"There are some recruits around here. Get them and bring them to the hideout."

Tor's brow shot up, and he looks between Sey and Sullivan. An understanding passes between them, and she nods.

Sullivan takes that as his cue and straightens his suit jacket. He gives one more look at Tor before climbing back in his car and pulling out of the alleyway. Tor doesn't breathe again until his presence is gone.

Tor takes a deep inhale and rolls his shoulders.

"What the heck was that about?" He asks Sey.

Sey runs her hands through her short, purple hair. Uncovering her almond-shaped eyes and exposing their shiny, onyx color.

"He has a plan. We just carry out the orders. You know how this works." Tor opens his mouth to argue, but Sey leaves him at the side of his car. Tor jogs after she catches her wrists.

"What, Tor?" she asks aggressively.

Something *was* horribly wrong, and it was about to get worse. He could feel it in his gut.

"Just let me in on what you think he might do. I have some friends who work at that club, and I'd like to keep them out of it, if at all possible." Tor says.

With a resigned sigh, Sey rummages through her car until she can pull a blue gun with a star-plated print on the handle out of her glove compartment.

"You see this?" she asks.

Tor nods.

"Use this to protect yourself. It's better than the Glock you have," she passes the gun over.

"Is he going to...kill them all?" Tor asks in a whisper. His voice cracks against his will.

Sey doesn't look up from the cushy pink cover over her steering wheel.

"What do you think?" she asks. She closes her door and buckles herself in.

The two of them stay in the same spot.

Her car rumbling to life breaks the silence. Tor puts her gun away and gets into his car.

Her headlights disappear, snatching away the light that danced across the building's surface.

Tor leans back into the seat of his car and closes his eyes.

'How to do this?'

Swallowing down his guilt, he turns the key, and his car rumbles to life.

When Tor pulls up to the strip club, a list of questions flies through his head.

What would they do when Sullivan popped up? What would they say? How would they look at him when they saw he'd betrayed them...again.

Tor steals his nerves and douses his thoughts in Vodka. The bitter liquid slouches around in his mouth and slips down his throat with ease.

He sits in the car waiting for the alcohol to take hold of his empty stomach. He closes the bottle and puts it in the passenger seat. Then he locks up.

Juice zips up his jacket before heading to the door.

"I hope whatever you've got going on here, don't getcha killed," he mumbles.

Tor pats his back.

"Thanks for letting me buy the place out."

"Buying the place without workers is not how this is supposed to work," Juice says with a sigh.

Tor smirks and waits until his friend is gone to leave for the back room. He steps in and looks around. Everyone was accounted for, even though he still failed to know their names.

Except for Luca. At least he was a friendly face.

"Where's the boss, mole?" asks a man in the back. Tor looks at him, at his shaggy hair and folded arms over his chest.

"He's on the way." Tor lies. He almost didn't believe how calm he sounded. His heart beat rapidly against his chest, and his hands shook slightly.

If Palo showed up and not Sullivan, he would probably puke.

He shakes his head and hovers by the door. Not knowing anyone besides Luca made him uncomfortable. He checks his watch.

'Shouldn't be too long now.'

The back door to the club slams closed, and several footfalls resonate against the club walls.

Tor stumbles back, resting his hand close to his hip.

No one says a word.

The door swings open. Several firearms point towards the Vipers as Sey pours in with the newbies.

The last person to enter is Sullivan, who carries a small suitcase with him. A shit-eating grin stretches across his face.

Whatever was in there was going to turn the tide, a foul odor follows the suitcase, the bottom stained with blood.

Ah shit.

Chapter Nine

Sullivan places his suitcase on the desk and turns to the Vipers.

Most of them glare between Tor and the South Sanz leader.

"Well, look at this. Some of the family is back together again." Sullivan says while looking specifically at the older Italian man with the cobra cane.

Luca holds his gaze, though there is no anger behind it, just pain.

Tor slips his gun from behind his back and divides his attention between the Vipers, who obviously want him dead, and whatever Sullivan has to say.

"What do you want?" One of the Vipers asks. Sullivan pops open the briefcase and twists it around.

Tor gags at the sight of the briefcase's contents.

He turns away shaking it off. When he gets his bearings back, he looks to the front of the room.

Inside the suitcase was a head, the bald head of an old Spanish man. Its eyes remained open, the mouth agape and dripping blood. The neck had been severed as if a sword had sliced it. There was only one person he knew who did that.

Rio de Cabeza, one of Sullivan's Right Hands.

'He really makes heads roll.'

Tor swallows uneasily. He'd have to be careful if he didn't want that to be his fate. His hands rub gently at his own throat.

Sullivan gazes around the room before lifting the head of his older brother into the air.

"You see, Palo here...he's a special man. He was once the successor of the Sanz, before someone better stepped up. Then he fled to become the successor of your little gang. How poor of taste for him to die at the hands of his brother, and be chopped to pieces by his *family*. How very unfortunate for him." Sullivan drops his head.

It hits the ground with a wet thunk. Standing on its neck. Blood spills from under it.

Tor's stomach lurches, and he holds back his nausea.

"I'll give you some options," Sullivan says. He raises a hand into the air, and one of the members at his side wipes the blood from his palm.

Sullivan stuffs his hands into his pockets once they are clean. "You can come with us, where you'll be treated as one of our own. Or you can walk away from life, forever."

One of the Vipers stands, raising his gun.

Several Sanz members point their guns at him.

Sullivan raises his hand to halt their fire.

"You fucking bastard. Why would we join your shitty gang?" The man curses out.

Sullivan sighs. He points at the head with his feet.

"You want to end up like him, Lance? With your head sent home to your father? Like a bouquet for your mother to smell, and water and admire?"

Sullivan passes through the room and takes hold of the gun. He places the barrel between his brows. "Then be my guest."

Lance lowers his gun. Tears spring from his eyes and race down his cheeks.

"Why are you doing this? You've already killed our whole gang. Both of our leaders, our friends, *la nostra famiglia*." Lance stutters out.

Sullivan lowers his gun.

"You misunderstand me, Lance. I don't kill anyone. They kill themselves." Sullivan says he clicks the safety on the gun and tosses it to Tor. Tor catches it and grips it tightly.

"I don't understand," Lance says, sniffling. His eyes have grown beyond his age, weary and tired.

"I've never targeted the Vipers; they've targeted me. Fought me for the way I run things, stole my turf, women, money, so I take back what's mine. And sometimes that means that I have to take more than what's mine. Because *some* people," He says, pointing behind himself. "Like to get *ahead* of themselves. Bite off more than they can chew, and that...gets them killed." Sullivan laughs at his own joke.

"He was your brother," Lance mumbles. His tears have dried up, and his voice has returned, albeit scratched up.

"No brother of mine wants me dead." Sullivan steps away from Lance and past the rest of the Vipers.

"Now, you walk out that door and never look back. Or you come with me." Sullivan says. He steps past Palo's head towards the door.

One of the newbies picks up the head and places it back in the suitcase.

Lance grabs one of the guns and lifts it.

A gun fires, and the room roars with motion.

Lance's head jerks back, and his body hits the wall. He slides to the ground, blood streaking after him.

The other Vipers are quick on their feet, shooting and dodging.

Tor manages to shoot his lucky shot, hitting someone in the chest, and he makes his way out of the enclosed room.

The only person to step out of the room is Luca. He straightens his purple suit and steps heavily on his cane.

Sey lowers her gun and smiles at him.

"It's good to have you back, Papa." He nods at her and frowns in Sullivan's direction.

Tor shakes off the adrenaline pumping through him. Anyone left in that room wasn't coming out.

'Poor Juice, he's gonna be so upset.'

Tor stashes away his gun and passes Sey her gun back. She takes it and swings an arm over his shoulders.

"You little rugrat. You had me scared for a moment." Sey mumbles.

"Why?" Tor asks her to walk with her to the front door.

"Your reflexes are slow today. I thought you'd get killed." She says honestly.

Tor winces.

"They aren't that bad." He says, though he wasn't too sure. Everything in that room seemed to be moving at turtle speed until people started shooting.

It takes that for him to remember the gulp of Vodka he had before going inside. On an empty stomach no less.

Sey joins some of the other members in front of a large black van.

What was up with their endless array of vehicles? He'd probably never know.

Tor walks up to Sullivan, who is finishing a discussion with the newbie, who is lugging around the briefcase.

"Good job, boy," Sullivan says.

"Thank you, sir," Tor says.

Sullivan looks past him at the Italian man.

"You know he's Tony's father, right?" Sullivan asks.

Tor glances back and watches Luca swagger up to them.

"Yes, sir. I know." Tor says. Luca looked upset. But Tor didn't blame him; he'd be upset too if the last members of his family were murdered in front of him.

The question of how he remained unscathed bugged Tor a bit.

"My old friend," Sullivan says. Luca nods grimly.

"It's been a while since I've seen everyone. How are the kids?"

Sullivan chuckles.

"Their doing good. Adelio and Tony are getting a surrogate finally."

"I heard. Are you excited to have a grandchild?" Luca asks, raising a brow. Sullivan leans against the van behind him.

"Not exactly, I'm too young for grandchildren."

Luca snorts and raises to his full height. He sticks out his hand, and Sullivan takes it. Their hands clap together, and they both give a firm shake.

"Welcome back. We're heading in, would you like to grab your wife?" Sullivan asks.

Luca nods. "I'll meet you there," he says.

Sullivan turns back to Tor. "Get your stuff. We're going home." Sullivan smiles a real smile, for once. Then climbs into the back of the van with the other members.

Tor stands there and waits for them to depart. Luca pats his shoulder, breaking him out of his thoughts.

"I'm glad you decided to join us," Tor says.

Luca shakes his head of gray hair. "Unlike Sulli here, *I want* to see my grandchild."

"S-Sulli?" Tor stutters, dumbfounded.

Luca leans against the cobra head of his cane, balancing from foot to foot.

"You don't call him by his nickname?" Luca asks. Tor shakes his head vigorously.

Luca shrugs. "You're missing out. It's a pretty funny nickname." Luca says. He then ambles off towards his car.

Tor stares in horror at the man.

Only old heads could get away with calling a monster like Sullivan, *Sulli*. It didn't even sound right in his head!

He scoffs and jumps in his car. He had some stuff to get.

The cleanup crew pulls into the strip club parking lot. They rush around in their yellow hazard suits, pushing carts of supplies.

Tor pulls off, back to his mother's house.

Chapter Ten

TOR GRABS HIS BAGS and puts them in his car. He makes the walk up to the house and looks around the yard. The snow had melted away, leaving a light covering of dusty white that remained stuck to the ground, trees, and the tops of cars that hadn't moved in a long time.

The light from the streetlight flickers on, and the rest of the street follows suit.

Tor steps back into the house and pulls his durag from his head. He plops it on the living room table and sits on the couch.

This would be the last time he was here until his mother left rehab. For a minute, and just a minute, he closes his eyes and remembers the fragments of his childhood.

The small hands that wound around his neck and squeezed as tightly as they would go. The small feet that just kept kicking. The voices that shouted incredulous things at the tops of their lungs. But nothing was as painful as when they stopped.

Tor rubs his chest under his collarbone. Beneath his coat and the thick cotton of his shirt is a tattoo. *God's Angel*. So boldly declared across his body.

He clutches the chains at the base of his neck. On his heaviest chain, he'd placed the image of his savior, a gold-encrusted emblem of The Most High.

He breathes in the scent of his childhood. A slightly warm, lavender scent, followed by sugary treats...and blood.

Tor opens his eyes and releases his clasp on his chain. He rolls his head about his shoulders and shakes the memories off his skin.

Every bit of this house was the same.

Obituary cards still littered the top shelf of the cupboard where the pretty china cups used to be, and under it was a box of toys his mother had locked away.

Under those was a gun, his father's gun that he'd left after he'd abandoned them.

Tor stands up and opens the cupboard. Maybe he could open the chest for once.

Tor tries the lid just to see, but it doesn't give away. Faced with his curiosity, he looks around the living room in search of the key.

There had to be a key; his mother never locked anything up for too long.

His look around the living room was unfruitful; there wasn't anything but an old bottle of Gin stored away under a box of DVDs. Tor stashes it to toss later and keeps looking around the house.

He steps into the kitchen and runs his hands over the scratches in the countertop.

He remembered so vividly that he could see, in the reflection of the kitchen window, a boy with angry blue eyes and a broken nose, dragging large kitchen knives across the countertop.

Tor looks back down at the deep indentations. The cuts he'd gotten from those knives had long since healed and turned to white flesh. Then he had them covered in inky black tattoos.

But faintly, if he looked, he could still see them.

One crossed just under the bed of his nail, and that streaked all the way across his hand from when he had lost hold of one of the knives. And the other, which cut deep into his palm, was the result of the way he'd clutched the knife as he dug his name into the countertop.

Tor tries to remember his punishment for etching into the counter, but he can't seem to, or for the sake of his sanity, he must have blocked it out.

Tor steps away from the counter and reaches around in the cabinets. Checking all the opened boxes, bags, and then re-closing them. He checks the counters and all the drawers, but he comes up empty-handed.

He stops before the sink mat. It was green and moldy from the splashing of water, the dirty shoes and feet that stepped on it, the paws of the stray animals, and the others that had taken in for a few months at a time. And dirty from the numerous drugs that fell on it, and the alcohol, which had splashed into it.

Tor lifts the edge of it with his shoe and kicks it over. Years' worth of dirt and grime ring around the shape of the rug. But there was nothing there, nothing under it.

Tor finds his mother's dishwashing gloves before picking the rug up and placing it back over the line of demarcation. He puts the gloves back where he found them and ventures further into the house.

If I were a key, where would I be? Tor thinks to himself. He goes upstairs to look in his mother's room and turns up empty. He wasn't in there often enough when he was a kid. He might have learned something useful that stopped him from the life he currently leads.

Tor knows it's not in his room.

His eyes flick up and down the hall at all the other doors.

He takes a deep breath and opens the first one.

The twins, his elder sisters. *Taiwo and Tana.*

Their room had been a haven for the boys when they were being too rough.

But it only lasted a short while, and his haven had fallen from a sanctuary to a hell.

Tor walks into the room. On one side, there is a bunk bed with satin sheets on each mattress. To protect his sister's natural hair. With pillowcases to match. The bonnets they laid out after making their beds were gone, off with them into the real world.

It smelled the same. Cinnamon and oily hair products. They were the first people to teach Tor how to do his hair. He'd grown it real long when he was a kid, down his back almost. He even dreaded it like Samson, but all good things come to an end.

Tor couldn't shake the memory of the fire that lit up his back and burned his skin and hair off. Tears spring to his eyes, and he gives himself a moment. Even as a child, when his brothers had set his hair on fire while he slept and he woke up in agonizing pain and fear, he could still feel just how cold and alone he really was.

Tor shuffles endlessly through the room, but nothing even shaped like a key is found in his search.

Tor opens the next door past the bathroom. His two older brothers, *Tommy and Taavi.* They often seemed like twins born a year apart with matching smirks and similar walks. They did everything in pairs and always had each other's backs. Even went to the same college. Tor finds an abundance of junk under their pillows. R-rated movies, keys to who knows what, bullets for their Nerf guns, firecrackers, packs of stale gum, pencils. Why anyone would sleep with a pencil under them is a mystery, but that's what was there.

He takes the keys, remembering to note which one belonged under what pillow. He's sure they wouldn't remember or wouldn't even care to check for them since no one came back. *No one but him.*

Tor rounds the mess of their rooms out into the hall for the last door. Since his room was downstairs and their father had slept in the room with his mother, he knew the last bedroom belonged to the youngest of his older siblings.

Turk and Tajara, these two numbskull's were definitely the weakest of his brothers. They were only a year or two apart from Tor and almost four years younger than Tommy and Taavi. Their room was immaculately cleaned as always. Since Tajara has OCD, and Turk...was just not sentient.

Turk was the worst one in a sense. Had no sense of self-gain or independence. He did whatever was asked of him, and it was normally holding Tor down while they took out their frustrations on him. Or telling him something inhumane. Turk's favorite insult seemed to be the real reason Tor suffered so much under this roof.

You weren't wanted; that's why Dad left because you're such a useless, helpless, annoying sack of meat.

Tor stares into the room, his gaze drifting almost far off in his mind. The alarm he'd set on his watch goes off, breaking him from his stupor. Tor shuffles around. Finding only one thing of interest.

The bible.

He opens to the marked page and instantly recognizes the scripture. It was the one tattooed on his chest, just like a bookmark.

John 3:16, For God so loved the world that He gave His one and only Son, that everyone who believes in Him shall not perish but have eternal life.

Tor puts the bible back and takes deep, steadying breaths.

One of the keys in his pocket had to work.

He descends the stairs to the living room and opens the cupboard. He pulls the chest from the shelf and sits on the couch. He tries three keys before one clicks in the lock. He pops open the chest and reveals all the toys that haunted his childhood.

If toys are what they would be called.

On top of the pile is a small square container with a glossy, wood finish. But when he flicks it open, fire dances in front of his eyes. This is what lit his hair on fire and burned his back all the way up his neck and the base of his scalp. Tor stashes the lighter, though he doesn't smoke.

He moves the kitchen knives to the table. They were dull and split at the tip from him dragging them through the counter, one even had faded, crusted blood on the sharp side. *His blood.*

Tor pulls out a slingshot and rolls it over his fingers. It was the one that Taavi filled with rocks and shot at his face.

Then the semi-automatic pistol his father wore at his hip in a holster.

He took it to protest at City Hall, or when he went to work at night. Even in Tor's most vivid dreams, he couldn't remember the man's face.

But he did remember the A-frame T-shirt and the light wash blue jeans he wore the day he left.

Most of all, he remembered his dark brown holster and the pistol sitting snug in it.

Chapter Eleven

WHEN TOR GETS OUT of his car, a chill runs up his spine. It's been a while since he made his way to the Armory, the Sanz gang's main headquarters.

He rolls his shoulders and steadies his nerves. Whatever was behind that door couldn't be worse than what he's already seen.

Tor walks up to the white fence and opens it, his shoes crunching on the gravel as he approaches the porch. The wind chimes on the porch gently twinkle in the cold air. The little house looked smaller.

He opens the door, which, from what he knew, remained unlocked. The hallway of the house was dimly lit, and a candle sat flickering on the table by the door. An apple scent wafted from it.

Tor takes off his coat and places it in the closet behind the door.

His shoes echo in the quiet hallway to the living room. Sey sits on the couch, thumbing through a magazine. She turns slightly and nods at him.

"Took you long enough." She says with a smirk, though her eyes remain on the nude model on the page.

Tor scoffs and rounds the couch. His hands sink into his pockets, and he learns forward.

"Unlike you, I had to grab all my stuff and lock up the house."

Sey briefly glances up at him.

"Yeah, I know. How was she, by the way?"

"My mother?" Tor asks, plucking the magazine from her hands and flipping through some of the pages. It was way more provocative than he had been prepared for. With a flush brightening his deep brown cheeks, he places the offending object back in her hands.

"She's good now. At least I hope, I'll check on her in person next week, but I'll call later when I get a chance."

Sey puts the magazine on the coffee table and pops up out of her seat. "Alrighty then, you should go see Sullivan."

Tor nods.

He exits the room quietly and lightens his footfalls on his way to the office.

The wall of the hall was littered with photos of the gang members. Some had passed, some had gone to jail, and others were positioned in new places.

It was insane to Tor, who'd only been here for a year, that this gang was big enough to spill out of Los Angeles and into the neighboring towns, cities, and states. Tor stops in front of the last photo on the wall.

He peers at it with indifference.

Jaamini and he sit together on the hood of his Volvo. She looked up at him in the last few seconds before the picture was taken.

It's cute, with her wearing his bulky jacket and a myriad of emotions on her face. Their hands were clasped together.

It practically gave her father a heart attack when Tony placed the framed photo on the wall.

Tor snickers, recalling Pinky's disgusted face when he spotted the photo.

The door at the end of the hall opens, and cool air rushes out. Tor looks up at Sullivan, standing in the doorway.

"You two look nice together," he says.

Tor offers a tight smile and joins Sullivan inside the room.

"I won't keep you long. But I think it's important I address what's happened here."

Tor takes a seat across from Sullivan. "As you know, you joined our ranks a year ago and have been very efficient and respectful. Actually, you're one of my best footmen,"

"Thank you, sir," Tor says.

"With that being said, I know you don't want this life. A kid like you only wants to take care of his business and live a low-profile life."

Tor doesn't agree or disagree, but his brows raise against his will.

"I just need one thing from you, and you're free to go." Tor's mouth gapes.

'He's letting me out of the gang?'

Tor clears his throat. "Sir? Can you clarify a bit?" He asks nervously.

Sullivan stands and leans on his desk. Very reminiscent of a certain someone.

"You took a job that you knew could get you killed. Blowing up that casino and leveling almost the entirety of the Vipers. That's good work, I won't ask you to repeat it. Killing thousands like that...I'm not heartless. This is a hard life." Sullivan says.

He sighs. His curly hair had grown more silver than brown, and the ringlets no longer fell around his face or bounced when he moved his head. His finely cut beard was scraggly and streaked with the same silver his hair had. His hard eyes were now simply cold.

"Killing is hard, my boy, and you've done a great service to the gang. The least I can do is set you up with a good severance package." Sullivan offers a smile.

It's small and barely reaches his eyes, but the sincerity is there.

Tor smiles back.

But something was off, and it wasn't Sullivan.

"You should probably say your goodbyes if you know what's good for you."

Tor stands up and offers a hand for Sullivan to shake. Sullivan stares at it for a moment before taking his hand and offering the same firm shake Tor remembers from his first day.

"Take good care of your mother, boy," Sullivan says. He plops down into his chair and straightens his suit. Tor nods and closes the door behind him.

So even Sullivan gets tired.

Tor looks around for Sey and comes up empty. He shrugs it off.

There is only one person he really wanted to see anyway.

Tor ascends the steps of the Armory and walks up to the door of her room.

Jaamini spins around on Rollerblades, bumping salsa through her headphones. She glides around, swaying side to side, circling the small perimeter. She drops low and then jumps into a spiral.

It was all quite a lot for such a small room on the second floor of the house. He steps inside anyway, leaving the door open. He passes the en-suite door. The closer he got, the more fluid her movements became.

Her arms raise and fall in tune with the quickly shifting beat. Her breaths are shallow and deep. Her head inclines to the left following her leg. Powerful calves the size of his arm help her jump into the air again and land at a low squat.

It looks eerily like ballet.

Before he can move again, a silver blade rushes through the air towards him. He dips, nearly dodging it.

Slunk.

Tor stands, chuckling. One fist grips tightly to the hilt of her dagger.

Jaamini glares at him and slips the headset from around her head to her neck.

Tor carries the weapon face down, walking it to her with a small smile.

"You're as beautiful as always, my love."

As soon as he reaches her arm's length, she grabs her dagger and slips it away.

Jaamini looks up into his eyes and swallows dryly.

"How's your mother?"

Tor's smile broadens.

"I did it. She's in rehab!" He exclaims, albeit a bit loudly.

Jaamini's cold glare slips away, and she releases her arms from their tight embrace around her chest, sighing again.

"That's good," she says.

The two smile at each other for a time before she breaks eye contact to stare at the floor.

Tor's eyes meet hers, but his gaze slips to her yellow roller blades.

It's impressive she can move like that in those death traps.

"Tor, I would have understood. *Heck*, I understand. You're my *novio*. I can't be mad for long anyway." Jaamini says.

"*Novio?*" He asks hopefully.

A small smile breaks out over her lips. "Yeah, you thought you could get away with thinking we weren't an item?"

Tor shrugs, taking his hands from his pockets and leaning in.

His breath ghosts over the shell of her ear, and he breathes in her earthy scent.

"I would have it no other way." He mumbles, and Jaamini chuckles, wrapping her arms around his waist and pulling him flush against her.

"Oh, but my dad is going to have a fit," she says as an afterthought.

Tor is quiet for a moment before humming and wrapping his arms over her waist.

"Then we'll deal when the time comes." Jaamini sighs into his shoulder. Her face snuggles his neck.

The two spin around to the light sounds of the rushing music in her headphones.

A throat clears, making them pull away. When Tor's eyes land on Pinky, he winces.

Tor stands straighter, raising his head at the man. Pinky sighs, stuffing his hands in his pockets and leaning on the balls of his feet.

"Good afternoon." Tor rushes out.

Silence fills the room, and the two men hold each other's gaze.

"You promised," Pinky says. He leans into the wall right where the wedge print of Jaamini's dagger was.

"I did. And I am to blame for all that came after." Tor says, straightening his shirt and jacket.

Pinky nods, turns away, and heads to the door.

"This is not going to be the last time we address this." He says before stalking out. His heavy boots pound on the steps as he recedes deeper into the house.

Jaamini and Tor share a knowing look.

Chapter Twelve

TOR LOOKS PAST HIS fingers to the light of the sun. Wind ruffles his jacket, and heat sinks into his skin. He breathes deeply the cool, fresh air of the mountain and closes his eyes.

Peaceful.

That's the word he would use to describe this moment in his life. But it was too peaceful. He pushes the negativity from his mind. He relaxes his muscles and rests on the dirt on his back.

Quiet.

That's the word he would use to describe the mountains. But it was too quiet. He grits his teeth and tries not to think about how undisturbed he is. His shoulders release their tension, and his fingers stop clutching the blades of grass beneath them.

Violence.

That was the word that kept seeping into his life up until this point. But it was never too violent, was it?

Tor frowns and opens his eyes. Violence followed him like a plague. From the moment his father walked out of his home, to this moment right here, sitting in the dirt on a mountain.

Violence was his driving force to survive. Kill or be killed, as some liked to call it, or a dog-eat-dog world, as his mother would say.

Tor closes his eyes again, trying to remember a day when something bad didn't happen. Where someone didn't fight, or die, or threaten his wellbeing, or the wellbeing of those he cares for.

His brows furrow, and his fingertips absently trace over the petal tattoos on his hands. Then he clutches the chain around his neck. He thinks, and thinks, and thinks. *Was there ever a day when he was at peace? Like this one.*

Tor opens his eyes and stares blankly out at the city far in the distance.

If he were a bird, he would face the daily fear of being eaten, yet he would remain content. He would stay perched in a tree with his wings folded at his side. He'd keep his eyes closed. Not because he would fly the same pattern every day, and see the same sights. But so he could listen to the wind, and the stories it held.

Tor closes his eyes again and listens. Not for real words, but for the sounds of the rustling branches. To the blades of grass that sweep softly against each other when the wind blows. To the soft chirps which grow steadier and louder as a flock of birds passes over his head. Something soft and velvety lands on his hand.

Tor opens his eyes and plucks the feather from the back of his hand. He twists it in his fingers and runs his thumb over its smooth texture. The bright yellow at the top of the feather faded into a stretch of black and ended in a white tip. The bird was quite common in Los Angeles, and the feather reminded him of Jaamini. He smiles and stands up.

His resolve grows with each step. Life with the South Sanz may be violent, but it was the only family he had besides his mother. It was the only life he knew, and knew it well. He'd promised his mother he would quit. This was it, his promise.

But promises like that were meant to be broken,

Tor gets in his car and leaves the mountainside to head into town. He knew what he wanted now. A family, a home, a place where everyone is one, and cares for each other so deeply. The gang is his *family*.

Tor pulls up to the Armory and steps out.

Jaamini argues on the porch with a man.

He'd seen him before, but he couldn't remember his name.

The sun was falling now that he had finally arrived, and their heated words told him all he needed to know.

The man towers over her, with his buzz cut and camouflage suit. A fresh and red scar dips under his eye and down his chin, like someone carved into his face. Tor closes the gate behind him, alerting the two to his presence. He doesn't stop walking until he's fallen in at Jaamini's side.

Tor leans down and kisses her temple. She offers him a slight smile.

"Is this him?" The man asks.

His dark eyes blaze with anger.

'There goes this peaceful day.'

Tor wraps an arm around Jaamini's shoulder. He holds it there lightly just in case he needs to move her out of harm's way.

"Yes, but it's really none of your business." Jaamini hisses out.

Tor raises a brow and looks between the two.

"Can I help you?" He asks the bulky man.

"This is Nico, and he was just leaving," Jaamini says. Her gaze is unnerving, blank and devoid of light.

She'd never looked like her father until that very second.

"No, I was not." Nico slurs. He turns his gaze back to Tor. "You don't understand what you're interfering with. So, unless you want to see stars, I advise you to leave."

Tor gently pulls Jaamini behind him. Enough for her to react as she pleased, but far enough for him to feel comfortable.

"Is that a threat?" Tor asks.

Nico grits his teeth and charges Tor with a pocket knife. Tor deflects his arm and punches Nico in the gut. Nico gets up and freezes in front of the barrel of Tor's gun.

"I don't want to hurt you, man. And I refuse to fight when it's not my fight." Tor says.

He frowns at the bloodshot look in Nico's eyes.

'Is he drunk?'

Nico stumbles into his next swing.

Tor kicks him down and shoots.

Nico cowers until he realizes the bullet had not hit him. Tor glares at the man for a long time.

"I won't kill you," Tor says.

"Shame," Pinky says from the gravel in front of the house. "You should be more willing to see that he is going to marry your girlfriend," Pinky says with a smirk.

Jaamini pulls Tor's arm down and shakes her head at him.

"What is he talking about?" Tor asks in a mumble.

Pinky ascends the few steps onto the porch and pulls Nico to his feet.

"This man is betrothed to her. This is Jaamini's future husband." Tor's frown deepens.

"Are you religious?" He asks Jaamini. She offers a half-hearted shrug.

"I'm not going to marry him," Jaamini says, looking at her father. "I'm going to marry Tor."

Pinky grits his teeth. Tossing the drunk Nico away from him.

Nico stumbles, catching on to the side of the house to stay standing.

Pinky stalks up to the two of them, noticing the looks on their faces. He pulls his shades off his face, revealing his bright eyes. They looked like Jaamini's, whereas his are only blue and not blue-green.

"You two aren't allowed. You do not have my blessing. Don't forget that he started in this gang as a mole." Pinky says, seething.

"And he's proved himself! Even Sullivan likes him."

"Sullivan is not your father," Pinky says and backs away.

"You are not allowed to marry this boy. Your marriage will come soon. So stop trying to avoid it."

Tor steps forward.

"Sir, I understand we got off on the wrong foot. But don't you think it's wrong to force your child into marriage? She's still so young."

"Shut the fuck up. You can't tell me shit about raising my child, and if you have any sense in that brain of yours, you'll end things quietly and in a timely fashion."

Pinky pulls Nico from the porch and down the gravel pathway and into his car. The tires screech when he pulls off.

Jaamini sighs deeply.

"I'm sorry, Tor. I just learned about this last night. I didn't have time to warn you."

Tor turns to her and grabs her hands.

"It doesn't matter. We'll fight this together." Tor says.

Jaamini smiles up at him.

Tor breaks away and fishes in his pocket until he finds the feather.

"Open your hand." He says. Jaamini raises a brow but opens it. He places the feather in it.

"It reminds me of you." Jaamini holds it up to the sky; its bright yellow color looks almost sunburnt in the glow of the porch light.

"Why?" She asks. Tor looks at it before looking at her.

"You are a whirlwind of color in my very bleak life. You make things bright again." He points at where the yellow meets the black and how it ends in white.

"Aw, you're so good with words," Jaamini says. Tor smirks.

Then his smile fades. "Oh yeah, I'm rejoining the gang."

Jaamini gasps and stops turning the feather around her hand.

"What do you mean, you're rejoining the gang?"

He pulls her into a tight hug.

"Oh, come on, you really thought I'd abandon my *familia*?" Jaamini stares at him with wide eyes. "Wow, I can't believe you really thought I was done. I can't blame you. I thought the same thing."

Jaamini snaps out of her stupor. "Why change your mind then?"

Tor shrugs his shoulders.

"Do I need a reason to stay with the people who've taken care of me for a year, and in turn, a lifetime?" He counters.

Jaamini shakes her head no.

"Well, then, come with me when I tell Sullivan."

Jaamini tucks the feather away in the pocket of her sweater dress and follows Tor into the Armory.

Chapter Thirteen

Tor takes Jaamini's hand and points her towards a jeweler.

They were out for some much needed retail therapy. Hell, this was the only therapy they could afford to do, any other therapist would have them locked up in a heartbeat.

"You said you wanted a new bracelet, right?" Tor asks.

Jaamini nods, and the two of them head through the mall to the store.

When they get inside, Jaamini beelines to the bracelets. Tor stops to look at the rings. He wasn't in the market for any...but it didn't hurt to see what was there.

He browsed some of the diamond rings, some of the topaz, and a few pink diamonds before one of the workers slid up to him.

"Looking for an engagement ring?" She asks. He shakes his head no. She raises a brow and looks over to Jaamini. She leans in closer and lowers her voice.

"A promise ring, then?" Tor takes his eyes off the racks and racks of rings and looks over at the woman. She plastered a smile on her face.

With a sigh, he nods. It didn't hurt to look, but if Jaamini asks him about it later, he was definitely going to deny such a thing.

The woman leads him further down the shelves of rings until the prices start to decrease steadily. The rings became less extravagant and sparkly, though they looked the same.

Tor shrugged at these rings. They weren't as great in his opinion.

Jaamini wraps her arm over Tor's and leans over him to look at the ring he is looking at.

"That's cute. You buying something for your mom?" She asks.

He eyed her; she sounded genuine, but he knew she was fishing for information. He hadn't forgotten what she said to her father.

Tor swallows back his discomfort and stands to his full height of six three. Jaamini clasps his hand in hers and pulls him along to the bracelets. He gratefully accepts the distraction.

The two select a strawberry-themed, gold bracelet adorned with amethyst stones. Tor pays for it while Jaamini looks at some other brackets. He passes the tiny bag to her, and she balks at it.

"This was expensive, why'd you get it?" She asks quietly, looking around.

"I can't get you jewelry?" Tor asks without answering her.

Jaamini smiles. "Of course you can, but I wasn't exactly expecting you to. Thank you." Tor pulls her into a tight embrace and turns them back to the bracelets. He feels a bit guilty for lying to her for so long. This was the least he could do to make it up to her. He'd never had the money before, and he sure as hell wasn't going to keep it for himself.

"Anything else catch your eye?" He asks. Jaamini shakes her head.

"No. We need to head back. I just got a text from Sullivan."

Tor nods. The two of them exit the store hand in hand. Meandering through the mall, knowing they should hurry up but couldn't seem to be bothered. Whatever was so important felt worlds away.

"How is it having Sullivan for an uncle?" Tor asks. Jaamini looks up from her boba tea and up into the sky. The air around them was warming quickly, and the frosty days were starting to linger behind them. Spring was taking forever to arrive, though Tor already missed the cold.

"Sullivan is fine. You know he's insane, right? He's absolutely bat shit crazy." Jaamini says. Jaamini and Tor snicker to themselves and get into his car. The car purrs to life, and they leave the mall, heading to the outskirts of town to the Armory.

"What do you think he wants?" Tor asks.

"He probably called us together to celebrate. He's like a strict parent. Do everything he says and jump to do it, but when it's all said and done, he likes to give out rewards for good behavior. The gang is like his children, every single one of them is important, but it takes a special kind of love and attention to keep them all in good order and well-behaved." Jaamini says.

Tor chuckles.

"Well, it'd be weird if we were his children. I mean the whole crew is made up of his niece and nephews, his wife, and his siblings, but I get what you mean."

Jaamini offers Tor a glare with no malice behind it.

Tor's phone buzzes in his pocket, and he fishes it out at a red light. He chucks it into Jaamini's lap.

"Can you check that for me?" He asks, pulling off as soon as the light turns green. They were a few blocks away now.

"It's Tony, he's telling us to drive faster because it's urgent," Jaamini says. She frowns and checks her phone.

"Even big cousin Adelio is texting me."

Tor risks a glance her way. Her brows collect together, and her eyes flick back and forth between the messages. Tor drives faster and pulls them up to the Armory. The two hop out and make their way inside. It was more packed than Tor had seen it since he first came here.

Every nook and cranny was jam-packed with members loading their guns or strapping up in vests. Nobody minds them as they push through the house until they find Sullivan and the Right Hands.

"What's going on?" Jaamini asks. Tor closes the door to Sullivan's office.

"An invasion," Sullivan says, simply tossing her a gun. Jaamini falls into place next to Pinky. Tor lingers by Adelio and Tony. "I've gotten word from an insider that the cops have been planning a stakeout for a while now, and now they're ready to make their move. So, we move too. I've got a mini-mansion prepared in San Jose. It's about time we head over there."

Tor swallows the bile in his throat. The only reason they'd have coordinates to this place had to have been Palo. Palo must have been tracking Tor much deeper than he thought. Now they were all in trouble.

"That's like a four-hour drive," Tony interjects.

Luca grabs his hand and shakes his head. "You think that Sulli is going to drive?" He asks with a chuckle.

Tony gapes at his father and turns to Sullivan.

"You're right there, old friend, we are headed to the airport, because I am not driving the whole way." Sullivan looks around at the faces in the room. Helena, his wife; Adelio, his son; Lucas; Tony; Jaamini; and Tor. Pinky, sitting behind his desk. And lastly, at Rio, who is leaning against the bookcase.

"Everyone in this room has a permanent place in this gang." He turns his eyes to Tor. "If you want it, or if you've *earned* it," Sullivan says and rolls his shoulders. "That means that even if we have to airlift your dead body, you're coming with us. We are a *family*. Do I make myself clear?" He asks.

Everyone affirms in their way.

"Good, go get suited up, we have a plane to catch," Sullivan says.

Everyone shuffles out of the room and into the numerous rooms, and then into the numerous shelves, closets, and boxes of weaponry. Weapons Tor didn't even know they had, including machine guns, sniper rifles, FR85s, grenades, flash bombs, and other items Tor didn't even know the names of.

He only takes what he knows how to use. Even though the sticky bombs aren't his pay grade, he picks them up, feeling he has enough experience blowing stuff up.

Once Tor feels adequately prepared, he makes his way to the Right Hands.

A few of them peer uneasily outside into the chaos. Cop cars have surrounded the area, and their owners hide behind them to avoid getting shot.

"We're heading out the side," Sullivan announces. Tor looks over at him, confused.

"But there is no side door." He says. A few people eye him, but others snicker.

"Who said we were using a door?" Sullivan asks. Tor eyes the side of the Armory wall. There used to be dozens and dozens of pictures of gang members, old and new, lining it. He hadn't even known of the wall's gray color, there were so many frames.

But now, he could see the empty, barren wall clear as day. Empty wall and an empty home.

One of the members backed away from his bomb masterpiece. *They're going to blow it up?*

Tor steps with Jaamini behind the rest of the Right Hands. Her dainty hand slips into his, and he nods at her.

They shift their body away when the small bomb detonates and step through the smoke out onto the lawn. Cops begin to shout and shoot at the people in the front in an effort to reach them.

The group, including several other members, filters behind the house into a parking lot. There were several cars parked, all black and shiny.

"When did we get these?" Tor mutters.

The rows and rows of them seemed to go on endlessly. None of them had license plates.

They walk past a good bulk of them until they get to the big SUVs that Tor remembers they always sent to pick someone up after a "mission."

"Isn't this hiding in plain sight?" He asks. Sey slaps his back and throws Jaamini the keys. He furrows his brows.

"Why's she driving?" He asks in a whine. Sey snickers before handing him two additional pistols from the stuff he had picked up.

"Because she doesn't shoot, at least not in this kind of distance." Sey answers before stepping into a car with Carter, another gang member he had grown close to over time.

Most of the gang seemed to be getting into cars of various shapes and builds. But they were all black.

'Who would the cops chase? Did it matter? Was that the point?'

Tor had several questions, but no one was available to answer them. Jaamini was just as confused as he was.

"Get in!" She calls from inside. He sighs.

They were doing this. They were running. Never in his time with the Sanz had they ever run from a fight; they always ended what they started.

Tor hops into the car.

'This fight. This is the last one.'

Chapter Fourteen

JAAMINI'S DRIVING SKILLS WERE debatable. She was getting better, but without an official license and just a few days of practice under her belt, she was hardly a getaway driver. But her shooting skills while moving were worse, so this would have to do.

Tor tries to focus on ducking when cops shoot at him. He blasts out their tires instead of trying to shoot them through their windows.

Another two go spiraling out of control and crash into each other, but four more take their place. Jaamini was speeding and swerving. Tor climbs inside, narrowly avoiding a few bullets.

"Jesus Jaamini relax. Just like we practiced," he says.

He tries his best to level his voice to something calm. But even he can hear the rasp of fear.

"I know. But there are just so many cars right now! We should have left earlier," she complains.

"Not really, we're in black cars. They're in white cars. In the night, if we turn our lights off, we have the element of surprise." Tor says.

"Driving with the lights off in the dark isn't practical," Jaamini says. Tor weighs his next words.

"I will drive at night," he says.

Jaamini flicks a glare his way.

Tor sighs and climbs back out through the sunroof. He knocks out three more tires before crouching down. Even if they weren't shooting, he would probably be crouching so that he could hold on to something. *She drives like a madwoman*!

Tor clucks and checks the sides of them. There were still plenty of Sanz members surrounding their retreat. He could almost make out Sey and her usual partner, Carter, through the thick, tinted, bulletproof windows.

Cars dart in and out, causing chaos. The regular people on the street beep and swerve out of the way.

Tor manages to hold on to the car and shoots another cop in their pursuit. He clicks both guns, and nothing happens.

The cop raises his gun and shoots. Tor dips back into the car and checks his arm.

He closes his eyes and breathes through his nose. The pain spikes through him fast and deep. His whole body grows hot, and weak.

"What happened? Did you get hit?" Jaamini asks frantically.

"No, my love," he says.

He glances at his arm again before reloading his guns. Tor steps out and focuses on holding his arms straight. Then he bends them just barely. Just enough to ease off the pain and not have to flex past what his muscles can handle.

He stands south paw and levels his shot. *Him or me*. Tor pulls both triggers. One bullet shatters the window, and the other hits the drive. The car swerves off the road and smacks into a building. Smoke rises from its hood, and another cop car emerges from it.

Tor clicks his guns and switches his attention to the other side. He had to thin out this herd or they were dead. Tor grits his teeth and shoots out the front tires of the car to his right, then does the same to the car on the left. Pain explodes in his left arm, and his hand drops on top of the car.

"Tor!" Jaamini calls.

"I'm alright, love." He calls back before emptying his clip.

Two cars crash into each other, and the explosion blocks the road.

Tor ducks down.

The sleeves of his jackets were singed.

He refills the pistols. These were his rounds before the last. He had to make them count.

He stands back up and shoots every cop he can see.

Sometimes he misses his arms growing heavy and weak. His ears were ringing from the loud blast, his hands were shaking, and he couldn't get a good shot.

"Shit." He whispers under his breath and shuffles around in his pockets. He dodges another shot coming his way before tossing the offending little black box behind their car.

The speed Jaamini is going is just fast enough for them to be out of range of the bomb as it detonates. He ducks from the explosion, and three cars fly into the air. One of them is a civilian car.

"Fuck." Tor hisses before grabbing another bomb and jumping up.

They were still coming like a flock of birds. Every time he got one or two, they would close in formation.

The passenger cop's shoot their guns at him, but they duck when they see the bombs he throws.

The one he tosses with his left side smacks onto the hood of a cop car, and they screech to a halt. The other bomb hits a parked car, and it explodes, tossing the other cops against each other.

Tor climbs back in, sighing. His legs were burning from standing and crouching for so long. He was haggard and thirsty.

"We are almost at the bridge," Jaamini says. He sits down and lets the fatigue seep into his skin. *Jesus, this is going to kill me.*

Jaamini swerves around a car that was flipped over and on fire. A man was trying to pull someone from the wreckage.

"Fuck, this is so bad," Tor finally catches the carnage around him.

He wasn't the only one doing collateral damage.

An older adult lay in the street holding someone's side while blood slipped down their face. A mother clung desperately to a child. People ran and screamed from the fire or the car crashes, with blood decorating their clothes.

Tor turns his eyes away and reloads his pistols.

'My life, or theirs.' He thinks again.

He sways when he stands. His body had grown numb and angry.

He breathes deeply and uses one hand to pop one tire off each of the cops coming. Two of them grind against each other and run off the road. Two more join the ranks from a side street. Tor checks his jacket. Three bombs left. One clip left.

He wasn't going to make it with just this. He felt behind him for the automatic weapons he'd grabbed. They were still cool and pressed into his waistband. He had backups, but he would need them for later.

"Tor..." Jaamini starts, he looks at her and then out the front.

Far off in front of them, cops were starting to accumulate.

They're going to block the bridge.

Tor stays silent. He had to take out what was coming. Jaamini glances at him. And her eyes zero in on his arm.

"You're hurt? Goddamn it, Tor!" She shouts.

"Just focus on the road, Jaamini." He says. "Do you have a gun on you?" He asks, knowing she wouldn't.

"There's probably one in the glove compartment."

Bullets ricochet off the window where he stands. Two cars from either side slam against them. Tor rolls down his window enough to stick the barrel of his gun out and shoot the driver. His hand jerks, and he drops his gun.

"Are you okay?' Jaamini rushes.

"Yeah, he shot my gun, and the kickback is challenging to handle." He makes sure the window is rolled back up before shuffling through the glove compartment. Jaamini shouts when their car is knocked into. Tor grabs the wheel and turns them into a spin, righting the car.

"Drive!" He shouts and climbs through the sunroof to shoot the two cops. He misses one and clips the other in the shoulder.

They were getting closer to the bridge. But as far as he could see, there weren't any Sanz members around them. They would need backup in a bit.

The cars at the bridge seemed just to keep piling as well. The whole LAPD was probably on call for this. Whichever cop cars had been in front of them had already crossed the bridge. About six cop cars block the bridge, with two sliding in place on either end. He only had three bullets left in his pistol. He takes out the gun from the compartment, a BFR .30/30. Revolvers weren't his style, but he popped a bullet into the gun.

Tor looks around, making sure to duck down for a moment. His eyes lit up, and he aimed. There was only one option he could think of. His stomach turns and twists as the truck emerges into the open.

"May God take mercy." He says before he takes a shot.

The explosion is instant. Fire licks up into the air, consuming it.

Tor cheers mentally. The explosion halts all but a few cars.

There were only two left.

He loads and aims his gun.

Chapter Fifteen

Jaamini yells at the sound of another explosion. This one was louder than the rest.

She groans as another police car swerves in front of them. She had already lost sight of the group. Jaamini knew she should have looked up the address on Google Maps.

"Tor!" She calls over the sounds of his shots. He ducks down into the car as it gets lit up with bullets. The windows were worse for wear; a few bullets were poking through stopped by the thick glass. It would only take a few more before they came crashing in.

He drops his empty pistols on the ground and climbs into his seat.

"This is bad, they've got us surrounded. I can't see Sullivan at all." Tor says.

"What do we do?" Jaamini asks. She may have sounded normal, but he knew she was freaking out. So was he. This was his consequence. He'd played the sides for too long and now it was bloodshed for everyone. Even the civilians.

Tor swallows down his nausea. He thinks to himself, while watching the cars behind him and the wastelands around them. There was no way out but on that bridge.

He inputs the address into the GPS.

He glances at Jaamini before making up his mind.

"Stop the car." He says.

"Are you insane?" she yells.

He shakes his head, no.

Jaamini watches all of the cops stepping out of their vehicles and crouching behind them.

They were going to get capped if they stopped.

Jaamini brings the car to a screeching halt.

Tor thinks for a minute. Just a minute, he'd been free too long. His consequences hadn't caught up to him until this moment.

What would his mother think when she heard about her baby on the news? Would they kick her out of rehab, even though he'd paid in advance? Would she relapse? Would Jaamini hate him forever for what he was about to do?

In a few minutes, they'll be thumping at the windows or staking out in the car.

Tor grinds his teeth.

'Think. Think'.

He looks at Jaamini, and she eyes him warily.

"Cut the engine."

She shakes her head no. Tor reaches for the key, and she tosses his hands away.

Her blue-green eyes pinned him in place. He breathes her in, his heart fluttering at just the sight of her. He was truly a fool, having taken for granted her presence in his life.

A fool gone mad.

His eyes land on the bracelet, the amethyst jewels sparkling in the fading sun.

"Love, I wouldn't do wrong by you."

Jaamini squeezes her eyes shut and cuts the engine.

Tor sighs and pulls her hands into his.

"I just want to show them we aren't going to shoot anymore." She nods.

Her grip on his hands remained tight, clutching at him with her life. The warmth of her hands makes him smile.

They'd been together for a while now, the best time of his life. She was his fresh air, his guiding light, his partner in crime, the love of his life.

And a horrible first-time getaway driver.

His hands were clammy, face feeling cold with sweat. Would he bleed out before he could save her? He didn't know and surely didn't want to find out.

He turns to his door and opens it slowly. He raises his bare, empty hands to the cops around them.

Tor steps out of the car. Jaamini mutters behind him.

The strong wind blows the scent of smoke, burning rubber and blood into his face.

Skid markers line the road behind them. Shells of bullets litter the ground.

But the water still flows, the birds still soar up above, and his heart still beats.

The cops don't lower their guns, but for the ones closest to him, he can see their arms relax. One of them starts speaking through a megaphone at him. He can't really hear the man over the sirens wailing behind him, or the blood rushing through his ears.

'They're coming.'

Tor's heart raced and pounded in his chest. His stomach rolled and flipped. 'This is going to be bad.'

Their car was boxed in by several police cars, with more on the way. He glanced back at Jaamini and shook his head. A few officers trained their guns on the windshield. Tor jumps into the car and leans into Jaamini's face; his hands clasp her soft cheeks. He doesn't hear the bullets passing by the door.

"Hey, you remember when we first met?" Tor asks suddenly.

Jaamini nods.

"Yeah, you were a waiter at Tony's restaurant."

"You remember how angry your dad was when we checked each other out, right?" Tor asks with a snicker.

Jaamini smiles, but it doesn't reach her eyes. She nibbles on her bottom lip and crushes the steering wheel under her calloused hands.

"Tor—" she says, her voice catching in her throat.

Every moment with her danced in his mind like a short story; a beautiful, blood-soaked story he couldn't change, and wouldn't dare.

"Come on, love, you know me. I'm good at this." He mumbles, resting his head on her shoulder. The moment his eyes closed, he felt his conscious slip.

She smelled like strawberries now.

When she arrived from Spain almost a year ago, she smelled like soil, warm fruits, and sunflowers. After all that time away from her home, she smelled like his home, like the city clung to her skin and poured from her hair.

His long finger twist one of her curls between them. They were smooth yet slightly frizzy.

"No, I just got you back. I don't want to separate again." She says with an exasperated sigh. Tears twinkle in those beautiful eyes. Her hands grip the steering wheel so tight the sound of bunching leather overwhelms his thumping heart.

Tor looks into her eyes. They were bright like the water in San Juan.

He chuckles lightly.

"Just for a moment." He says and points at two of the cars narrowly parked in front of the bridge entrance.

Jaamini shakes her head wildly. She could see what he meant about the formation, it looked breakable. Escapable.

"I'm not leaving." Jaamini stresses. "You're coming with me. Or so help me God."

"Take care of my mother until I get back."

"Tor," Jaamini warns and re-clicks the locks to the door. They were already locked, but she insisted on making it clear that they were in this together. They were partners, and partners did not leave each other to die in the arms of an enemy.

"Just go, baby," Tor says and swings his door open in one fluid movement.

He raises his empty hands while he steps out.

"Tor!" Jaamini yells, pulling his arm. Tor shakes her off and closes the door.

He catches her door open and rushes to the driver's side. He pushes it back closed and looks at her through the window. Jaamini's tears catch his attention, but he can't let her know that. She shakes her head, mouthing words he refused to read.

Someone has to be a distraction, and he needed to be the one.

All of this was bigger than him, but without his interference it wouldn't have happened this way. Without his disloyalty, the Sanz would still be drinking away in their little home from home, with their family.

Thankfully, the cops continue to shout at him instead of shooting. He needed this chance, one shot to save a life. Even if it was just hers.

His mask slips into place, and he smiles.

The car purrs to life, and all the police officer's flinch.

As the barricade became more rounded, they ran to hide behind it, then pointed their guns behind their shields.

"Goodbye, love." Tor mumbles as the car peels off and makes a sharp turn for the loose cars in front of the bridge.

Bullets whiz past his body and around his head as they shoot and try to stop the car. Tor turns, reaching for his gun.

"For the Sanz."

He pulls the machine gun from behind his back, from under his jacket and opens fire.

The sounds of the shots ring in his ear.

His body jerks and jostles from the force of bullets hitting him. In his back, arms, and legs. The air around him is stuffy with gunpowder.

He drops several of the officers in front of him and a few behind him. He manages to take a shaking hand and toss a flash bomb above his head.

The bang throws his equilibrium, and he drops to his knees.

His blood decorates the ground like shadow wings, as he empties his clips.

Jazmin
Galloway

THE LIMPID SERIES

Espresso Shot

About the Author

JAZMIN GALLOWAY SPENT HER childhood in New York with her nose in a book. Fiction and nonfiction alike, she has always been an avid reader. She has never been able to hold herself back from the ever-changing lands of the stories she tells. Galloway uses her work as a voice, shouting her stories out loud to the world.

If you are able to, leave a review. It is the best way to help new authors, as well as established authors, get their book seen by readers like you. Thank you.